All hell broke loose

The Executioner dove behind the Wrangler, drawing the Desert Eagle as he hit the ground. A split second later he was on his knees bracing the huge pistol on the Jeep's hood.

He spotted an AK-47 swinging his way. He ducked behind the vehicle a microsecond before a rifle round sailed over the Jeep. Moving low behind the engine block, Bolan leaned around the grill and brought up the Desert Eagle. A .44 Magnum bullet drilled through the nose of the submachine gunner.

He paused, knowing that if he could stay alive until the gunfight was over, the Mexican and American drug dealers would do his work for him and kill each other off.

There was a flaw in that plan however. And it was a big one.

MACK BOLAN

The Executioner

The Executioner®
Don Pendleton's
HOSTILE CROSSING

A GOLD EAGLE BOOK FROM
W⦿RLDWIDE®

TORONTO • NEW YORK • LONDON
AMSTERDAM • PARIS • SYDNEY • HAMBURG
STOCKHOLM • ATHENS • TOKYO • MILAN
MADRID • WARSAW • BUDAPEST • AUCKLAND

First edition April 2006
ISBN 0-373-64329-2

Special thanks and acknowledgment to
Jerry VanCook for his contribution to this work.

HOSTILE CROSSING

Printed in U.S.A.

Under the sky there is no uglier spectacle than two men with clenched teeth and hellfire eyes, hacking one another's flesh; converting precious living bodies, and priceless living souls, into masses of putrescence useful only for turnip-manure.

—Thomas Carlyle, 1795–1881
Past and Present

Greed sees a price put on the heads of some men and no value placed on the souls of others. I would gladly let the devils bleed each other dry, but too often the innocent are put in harm's way. I will continue to protect the lives of good people. Their souls are worth fighting for.

—Mack Bolan

THE
MACK BOLAN

LEGEND

Nothing less than a war could have fashioned the destiny of the man called Mack Bolan. Bolan earned the Executioner title in the jungle hell of Vietnam.

But this soldier also wore another name—Sergeant Mercy. He was so tagged because of the compassion he showed to wounded comrades-in-arms and Vietnamese civilians.

Mack Bolan's second tour of duty ended prematurely when he was given emergency leave to return home and bury his family, victims of the Mob. Then he declared a one-man war against the Mafia.

He confronted the Families head-on from coast to coast, and soon a hope of victory began to appear. But Bolan had broken society's every rule. That same society started gunning for this elusive warrior—to no avail.

So Bolan was offered amnesty to work within the system against terrorism. This time, as an employee of Uncle Sam, Bolan became Colonel John Phoenix. With a command center at Stony Man Farm in Virginia, he and his new allies—Able Team and Phoenix Force—waged relentless war on a new adversary: the KGB.

But when his one true love, April Rose, died at the hands of the Soviet terror machine, Bolan severed all ties with Establishment authority.

Now, after a lengthy lone-wolf struggle and much soul-searching, the Executioner has agreed to enter an "arm's-length" alliance with his government once more, reserving the right to pursue personal missions in his Everlasting War.

Prologue

United States Border Patrolman Sam Becker opened the door to his vehicle, slid behind the wheel and twisted the key in the ignition. As the air conditioner came on—spitting out air he'd often described as "hotter than the devil's breath"—he unbuttoned the front pocket of his uniform blouse and pulled out the CD *Herb Alpert—Definitive Hits*. Beads of sweat rolled down Becker's face as the air slowly cooled. But the sounds of the Tijuana Brass beginning "The Lonely Bull" made him smile anyway.

Becker backed out of his parking space along the side of the Laredo station, then pulled out onto the street. Soon he was making his way through the side streets of the South Texas border town and crossing the road that led south to the bridge linking Mexico with the United States. He drove on, finally coming to Interstate 35, the highway that split the U.S. in two and led all the way from Mexico to Canada.

"The Lonely Bull" ended and Alpert and his Brass started up with a remastered version of the "Mexican Shuffle." Putting a CD player in his government unit was strictly prohibited in the policy manual. But Becker had waited until he was only three months short of retirement before installing it. Several of the supervisors had ridden with him since then, and none had said a word. So with today being his final day on the job he had to figure he'd gotten away with it.

As he pulled up the on-ramp to the interstate leading north, Becker thought back over his career. He wasn't likely to go down in the Border Patrol history books. But he'd served his time, done his job and had nothing to be ashamed of. He'd even survived a couple of gunfights, which he'd never mentioned to his wife. And he'd earned the nickname "Iron Guts" Becker during his rookie year when they'd come across the swollen, half-eaten body of an illegal who'd died in the desert. Even some of the old-timers had found themselves chucking their insides out when they'd seen that. But Sam Becker hadn't.

Now, on what he suspected would be his final call as a U.S. Border Patrolman, he felt a lone tear run down his cheek to mix with the sweat still on his face. Iron Guts Becker was alone. He'd spent thirty years answering routine calls like this one, and if he wanted to get sentimental about it and cry he decided he could just damn well do so.

He'd have it out of his system by the time he arrived at the site, anyway.

Becker wiped his face as he drove on. Fellow Patrolman Ernie Hernandez had radioed in earlier, advising Laredo that he was stopping to check on a tractor-trailer that had broken down on the side of the highway. When Hernandez hadn't checked back in an hour later, Becker had been sent to see what happened. *Nothing* more than likely, Becker thought as he wiped his eyes again. The air currents in South Texas could play hell with a radio when they wanted to. Sometimes you couldn't pick up a transmission from one car to another across the parking lot. Other times you'd get snatches of conversation from the Texas Ranger's office as far north as Wichita Falls.

Becker came to the top of a hill and saw the eighteen-wheeler on the northbound shoulder of the roadway, a half-mile in the distance. The bright yellow Mexican truck license tag glowed in the sun, and the Border Patrolman chuckled to himself. There had been a time—before the North American Free Trade Agreement—when Mexican tags were all but unheard-of on this side of the border. Now such licenses were second only to Texas itself. He squinted into the sun, trying to make out the bumper sticker pasted just below the tag. As he neared, the letters came into focus: *Voto Martinez Para Presidente!* Vote Martinez for President. Becker reminded himself that an election was taking place only a few miles south.

Slowing as he drew abreast with the truck in the opposite lane, Becker was only slightly surprised not find Hernandez's unit parked to the rear of the big vehicle. Hernandez had more than likely driven the truck driver into town to arrange for a tow.

Becker switched off the music, lifted the radio mic from its clip on the dashboard and called in his position to the Laredo station. He frowned when confirmation of his transmission came back without even a hint of static. Had the shifting airwaves really been the reason no one had been able to reach Hernandez for over an hour now?

For the first time since leaving the station, Becker felt the mild uneasiness that always came over him when things simply didn't stack up quite right.

Becker told the dispatcher where he was and ended the call as he pulled in behind the trailer. The tingling on the back of his neck continued. He switched off the ignition and unfastened the retaining strap on the holster attached to his Sam Browne belt. Something just flat out wasn't right. He didn't know what it was, and he didn't know how he knew it. But it wasn't.

Becker exited the vehicle, closing the door quietly behind him. The first real evidence that something was amiss was the blood on the asphalt at the rear of the trailer. His eyes rose, and he saw more blood splattered across the closed doors to the trailer. He pulled out his SIG-Sauer. The patrolman stopped for a moment, his eyes taking in all they could while he was still in position to duck back behind the engine block of his own unit. But he saw nothing else.

Slowly, Becker made his way to the cab. Halfway there, he called out. "You! In the cab! Come out with your hands up. Now!"

When a full sixty seconds brought no response whatsoever, he made his way to the door. With a deep breath, he lifted himself up toward the driver's side and peered through the window, the weapon at the ready. The cab was empty. The curtains separating it from the berth behind were open, and the mattress was empty as well.

Becker made his way back to his car and radioed for backup. He had just completed the call when a soft moan came from the tall grass to the side of the shoulder. Pistol leading the way again, he moved carefully down the embankment, only then noticing that a faint trail of blood led that way from the larger pool at the rear of the tractor-trailer. Halfway down the hill to the ditch, he saw patches of khaki and green through the yellow grass and straw.

The same khaki and green he himself wore.

Hurrying now, Becker reached Hernandez in time to hear his fellow Border Patrolman draw his last labored breath. It looked as if the man had taken a full load of buckshot to the face. Eyes, nose, ears—all of the features were gone, and it was a wonder that Hernandez's brain had lived long enough to send out the moan.

Becker turned away from the body, shaking as he walked back up the embankment. Even in the hundred-degree heat he felt cold—as if he was walking through a deep freeze. The sweat had frozen to his face and arms, and his hand had grown stiff and felt paralyzed around the gun.

What had this been over? What was the truck carrying? Drugs?

Reaching the rear of the trailer again, Becker stepped carefully around the pool of blood, the gesture done more out of respect to Hernandez's memory than any fear of contaminating the crime scene. Reaching up, he grabbed the latch holding the twin doors, twisted it and swung both doors open.

The smell was what hit him first. Bodies decayed quickly in such heat, and the nineteen Mexican men and women who had planned on crossing the border to a new life had, instead, ended their days in the back of this stifling trailer. Flies and other insects had found their way through the cracks and crevices, and buzzed throughout the giant coffin as they feasted on the rotting flesh.

Becker felt himself involuntarily backing away, his vision fixated on the face of a young woman staring sightlessly back at him with one open eye.

Iron Guts Becker ended his career with the Border Patrol puking his lunch over the hot, tarry asphalt.

1

"The bottom line is, if you try to run, or double-cross me, I'll kill you."

The head of the man behind the wheel of the Jeep Wrangler bobbed nervously up and down in acknowledgment. By the light of the full moon the big man saw a knot in the dark-skinned throat, as if the Mexican were trying to swallow a baseball.

The Wrangler had just left the border town of Reynosa, Mexico, heading southwest toward Monterrey. Traffic was light, and Mack Bolan settled back in the passenger's seat for the drive, mentally going over what had happened in the last few whirlwind hours.

Frederico Lopez, now behind the wheel of the Jeep, had murdered a U.S. Border Patrolman after the truck full of illegal aliens he'd been driving broke down north of Laredo. Leaving his human cargo to die in the sweltering heat, Lopez had escaped in the Border Patrol car and driven it back to the border. There, less than a block from the bridge linking the two countries, and in full view of the U. S. Customs officials in their booths, he had foolishly parked the high-profile vehicle and attempted to return to Mexico on foot.

By then word of Ernie Hernandez's murder, and the nineteen other corpses found inside the tractor-trailer, had been blasted across every police-band radio in Texas. Somewhat in awe, the U.S. officials had watched Lopez, wearing blue jeans and a T-shirt rather than the USBP uniform, exit the vehicle, then attempt to mix in with a group of American tourists crossing into Mexico. Lopez had been taken into custody without incident.

The moon seemed to glow brighter as the Jeep left Reynosa behind, illuminating the semidesert-semiprairie lands around the highway. Bolan pulled a bandanna from the front pocket of his jacket and mopped sweat from around his neck. The air was stifling and even the breeze created by the Wrangler's movement was hot, intensifying the heat rather than relieving it.

Bolan watched Lopez out of the corner of his eye. The man was a mass murderer as far as he was concerned, it was tempting to just have him pull the Jeep over and put a bullet in his head right now. But Lopez, facing multiple death sentences, had become anxious to help authorities the very moment he was arrested. He had given up the fact that he was a low-level illegal immigrant smuggler—a coyote—within the Jimenez crime organization, a Mexican syndicate known to smuggle everything from migrant workers to drugs, diamonds and antiquities. But what interested the Executioner most was little more than a rumor Lopez had overheard.

A big operation involving high-tech, next generation arms was about to go down along the border between the Jimenez group and some American dissident faction. Lopez didn't know who the Americans were, and he didn't know what the weaponry entailed. But the Jimenez group had been busy gearing up for the deal for several weeks.

As they bumped up and down out of chuckholes in the ill-kept highway, Bolan reached under his unbuttoned jacket. Beneath it, he wore only a black tank top, and as they topped a slight rise the Executioner's fingers slid across the damp cotton to the butt of the Beretta 93-R under his left arm. Screwed onto the threaded barrel was a sound suppressor, which quieted the noisy weapon to a mere whisper.

Bolan and Lopez remained silent as the Wrangler descended the other side of the hill it had just climbed. Satisfied that the Beretta was in place, the big man made a quick check of the extra magazines hanging under his right arm, then dropped his hand to his belt. His mammoth .44 Magnum Desert Eagle rode on his hip in a custom-made holster. The formfitting plastic held the weapon securely, and eliminated the need for a further retention device of any kind saving a fraction of a second in draw time.

And life and death, the Executioner knew, was measured in those fractions of a second.

Just behind the Desert Eagle, also attached to his belt and concealed by his jacket, rode two extra magazines of .44 Magnum ammunition. One had been loaded with 240-grain semijacketed hollowpoint rounds for maximum knockdown power. The other held needle-nosed full-metal armor-piercing rounds for maximum penetration. At the small of his back, clipped inside his pants was a TOPS Special Assault Weapon. The knife's tanto tip could easily be stabbed through a car door or hood, and the no-nonsense skeletonized handle cut down on both bulk and weight.

"How much farther?" Bolan shouted over the wind whipping through the Jeep.

Lopez shrugged. "Three, maybe four miles," he shouted back.

Conversation was difficult in the open air Wrangler, but the Executioner wanted to go over their story one more time. "Tell me again what you plan to tell Sanchez," he shouted.

"I have told you ten times already," Lopez shouted back.

"So make it eleven," Bolan said. "You're not the sharpest knife in the drawer or you wouldn't have driven the Border Patrol car almost onto the bridge before getting out."

There was a moment's pause during which Bolan saw the driver flinch at the insult. That was fine. Lopez needed to be reminded who was in charge. And he needed to be reminded that he was facing twenty counts of murder when he returned to the U.S. It had taken some smooth talking from Hal Brognola, the Executioner's longtime friend and contact in the Justice Department, just to get Lopez out of jail in the first place. And if the man now driving the Wrangler stood a chance of serving life in prison instead of soaking up a lethal injection, he would have to lead Bolan up the chain of command of the Jimenez crime syndicate. *Before* the high-tech weaponry had a chance to cross the border into American criminal hands.

Lopez shouted, "I tell Ricardo that Jimenez decided to send us at the last minute. That there is something about this deal with the American that he doesn't trust."

Bolan nodded.

"But I still say, as I have said before, it will look very strange to Sanchez if I am not armed."

The Executioner wasn't surprised. Getting a gun had been a theme Lopez had driven into the ground since their first meeting a few hours earlier. But it wasn't so he wouldn't look strange to Sanchez. Lopez wanted firepower so he could shoot Bolan in the back at the first opportunity and escape deeper into his native Mexico. He was a man, after all, who had not only murdered a Border Patrolman but had left nineteen of his fellow countrymen to die a slow and grueling death from heat exhaustion in the back of a tractor-trailer.

"He will wonder why the face he does not know is carrying guns and the one he recognizes is not," Lopez reasoned.

"You know," Bolan said. "I think you're right." In the moonlight, he could see the shock on Lopez's face as he twisted in his seat and unzipped the canvas gear bag in the back of the Wrangler. "A .45 okay with you?"

Lopez still looked surprised as he said, "Certainly."

"Good," Bolan shouted over the wind. "Then I'll get it ready for you." From the corner of his eye he saw the smile on Lopez's face turn into disappointment as he removed the magazine from the weapon, flipped the seven rounds out with his thumb, then worked the slide to eject the round already in the chamber. He tossed the cartridges out of the Jeep onto the highway.

Reinserting the empty magazine into the .45's grip, he handed it to Lopez. "Now you won't look strange at all," he said.

Lopez mumbled something unintelligible as he took the weapon and jammed it into his belt.

The two men fell into silence again as they continued down the highway. Bolan reevaluated the situation they were about to face for perhaps the one-hundredth time. Every plan had its potential problems, and this one was no exception. They weren't going into the deal completely cold but they were definitely chilly. In his low position as a transporter of illegal aliens for the Jimenez organization, Lopez barely knew Ricardo Sanchez, the Jimenez man who was doing the drug deal tonight with the unidentified gringo. Which meant Sanchez would likely be surprised to see a barely known face and a completely unfamiliar one show up.

Whether Bolan and Lopez were welcomed with open arms or bullets remained to be seen.

As the Wrangler moved on and the wind whipped through both men's hair, Bolan turned to the driver. "This drug deal tonight," he shouted over the noise. "With Americans. Are they the same Americans getting the high-tech weapons down the line?"

Lopez shook his head and blew air out between his clenched lips. "I have told you over and over and over," he shouted back. " I *do not know.*"

The Executioner didn't respond. He knew he'd asked the same question multiple times—that's what you did with informants you didn't trust. Sometimes, if you asked it often enough, you eventually got a different answer. And once in a while, you even got the truth.

The Jeep suddenly slowed and Bolan saw a billboard ahead on his side of the road. Just below the sign, someone had stapled a rectangle of cardboard reading *Martinez Para Presi-*

dente! It reminded Bolan that the Mexican presidential election was in full swing, and into the last couple of weeks. Challenger Julio Martinez seemed to gain several poll points a day over the incumbent running on a reform platform. He was claiming that he wanted to clean up the entire Mexican government.

Lopez twisted the wheel past the sign, and they began winding their way down a road that was as much prairie grass as dirt. The Executioner estimated they had driven roughly a half mile from the highway when a set of headlights blinked off and on three times in the distance. Lopez slowed further as they neared, then pulled to a halt ten feet in front of the lights. They belonged to an old and rusting Ford pickup. Behind the pickup, Bolan could see two other vehicles. The nearer one was an ancient Dodge Dart. The other was a seventies-era Camero with nothing but gray primer paint covering its body. Both cars were empty.

But at least a dozen men suddenly emerged from the shadows to surround the Wrangler. All held the buttstocks of shotguns or assault rifles to their shoulders.

And all of the barrels were aimed at Frederico Lopez and the Executioner.

Lopez threw up his hands. "Hey, Sanchez!" he cried out. "It is me, Frederico Lopez! I have been sent by Jimenez!"

A short, powerfully built man wearing soiled khaki work pants and an equally dirty khaki shirt stepped out of the shadows and into the light on Lopez's side of the Jeep. A white scar that looked to have come from a knife started at his left ear and ran down his face, through his thick curling handlebar mustache and bottom lip, then off his chin. In his arms, he cradled a stubby sawed-off double-barreled shotgun.

"Put your hands down, you fool," he said.

Lopez relaxed.

"We thought you were *federales*," Sanchez said.

A nervous, almost girlish giggle escaped Lopez's lips. "You have not paid the *federales* to stay away?" he asked.

"Of course we have," Sanchez said. "But there are always those who cannot be bought. Or those who take the money and then cause trouble anyway." The muscular man's eyes rose from Lopez to Bolan. "Who is this?" he demanded. "I have not met this gringo before."

"He is new," Lopez said quickly. "Jimenez hired him less than a week ago." He paused to catch his breath. But his frightened words still came out raggedly. "He can be trusted, of course. Jimenez does not make mistakes when he checks men's backgrounds."

"Can the gringo not speak for himself?" Sanchez asked. "Did Jimenez hire a mute?"

The comment brought a round of laughter from the rest of the men still covering the Jeep with their rifles and shotguns.

"The name's Cooper," Bolan said. "Matt Cooper."

Sanchez dropped his eyes back to Lopez. "He looks capable," he said. "But why would Jimenez send *you*?"

The obvious insult brought another round of snickers from the men circling the Wrangler. Lopez ignored it. "Señor Jimenez has some misgivings about the gringo you are about to do business with," he said. "He sent us to tell you to be wary. And as added support."

The Executioner could see that the man found the story highly suspicious. But he nodded, then waved an arm behind him. The men around the Jeep lowered their weapons. Another wave of the arm invited Bolan and Lopez to exit their vehicle.

In the distance, several coyotes howled an eerie chorus as the two men got out. Sanchez circled the Jeep to the Executioner. "You are armed?" he asked.

"It's hard to shoot people if you aren't," Bolan said.

"Ah," said Sanchez. "A gringo with a sense of humor. I like that."

The Executioner shrugged. "Look, like the man said, Jimenez just hired me. And he teamed me up with Lopez to come down and back you up on this deal." He paused for a moment. The weak part of their story was that Sanchez already had plenty of men. And Bolan knew it would look better if he acknowledged that fact himself rather than let Sanchez or one of the others bring it up.

"Don't ask me why," he said. "It looks to me like you've got plenty of guns here already. But I'm the new kid on the block. I didn't think it was my place to question Jimenez on his distribution of labor."

Sanchez looked up into the Executioner's eyes, studying them for several seconds. But it was impossible for Bolan to tell if he had truly bought the story or not.

Lopez broke the ice. "Where is the gringo who is buying the…" His voice trailed off.

"Coke," Sanchez said. "He is buying cocaine. And I do not know where he is. He is late."

Just then a flash of light appeared in the distance, on the same dirt-grass path Bolan and Lopez had driven a few moments earlier. As the light neared, it broke into two parts, and when it got even closer the Executioner could make out four distinct headlights. Two vehicles. One right behind the other. And the headlights of the lead vehicle were much farther apart than those of the one following it. A truck perhaps.

A minute or so later, the question in Bolan's mind was answered as a black civilian-market Hummer took shape under the full moon. The vehicle behind it was a Suburban. Usually considered huge, it looked almost like a toy behind the military transport vehicle.

Both the Hummer and the Suburban ground to a halt behind the Wrangler, and the Executioner was slightly surprised when ten men got out of the two vehicles carrying weapons similar to Sanchez and his men. It wasn't the weapons or the number of men that seemed out of place. It was their clothing.

Instead of the jeans and T-shirts, or camouflage fatigues Bolan would have expected, the men who now advanced looked like they might have just come from a college fraternity mixer. Most wore short-sleeved polo shirts with designer emblems. A few were clad in jeans, but the rest walked forward in pleated casual slacks. Covering most of the feet that stepped into the headlights were expensive loafers. A few of the young men wore the latest in athletic shoes, which went well into the three-figure range of cost.

Bolan watched them as they came to a halt. All were in their early- to midtwenties, and could easily pass as college students crossing the border for a drunken night on the town.

He had to guess that was the image they were shooting for in order to take the customs officials' minds off drugs when they crossed back into the U.S.

A sandy-haired man with a Browning Hi-Power stuffed into his belt stepped forward. "You Jimenez?" he asked bluntly.

His words brought yet another round of laughter to the Mexicans. Then Sanchez asked, "Are you Pentad?" and they laughed some more.

The Executioner frowned inwardly. Pentad? What kind of name was that? It meant five and was undoubtedly some kind of code name for whoever was behind the fraternity boy coke buyers. But it had a familiar ring to it as well. But he didn't have time to search for details at the moment.

The sandy-haired man was chastened as he said, "Okay. Fine. Dumb question. Bosses don't show up for deals like this.'

"You are very wise," Sanchez said, the smile still on his face.

"You got the coke?" the American asked.

"We have it. Do you have the money?"

"Of course." The blonde twisted at the waist and nodded to another of the preppie-dressed drug dealers. The man turned without speaking and returned to the Hummer. At the same time, Sanchez pointed toward the rusting Ford pickup, and one of his men took off for the vehicle. The two couriers returned to the scene at the same time. The Mexican carried a green duffel bag. The American had a leather briefcase.

"Brain Boy!" the American called out, and a small man wearing thick wire-rimmed spectacles came forward. Squatting on the ground, he pulled a black leather case from his back pocket and opened it to reveal several test tubes. The Sanchez man who had brought the duffel bag reached into it and produced a tightly wrapped package. Through the clear plastic wrap, Bolan could see the packed white powder. The Mexican handed it to the one called Brain Boy, who withdrew a small pocketknife and made a tiny slit in the pocket. A moment later, he had opened one of the tubes, dropped a small amount of the powder inside, recapped it and shook it up and down.

Bolan saw the man frown, then whisper something to the sandy-haired leader. Now it was the American leader's turn to frown. "It appears there's been some mistake," he said in a voice of controlled anger. "We were promised ninety percent pure. This is barely fifty percent."

Sanchez smiled and shrugged. "So we stepped on it a little," he said nonchalantly. "Mexico is a poor country. We must share what little wealth we have." Behind him there were a few more chuckles from his men.

"Well," said the blond man, "America is a wealthy country because we only pay for what we get. You cut the product by forty percent. That means we cut the money by the same amount." Opening the leather briefcase, he began pulling out packs of hundred-dollar bills, which had been wrapped with brown-paper bands.

He stopped when Sanchez aimed the sawed-off shotgun at his face and pulled both triggers at the same time.

The barrel of the shotgun had been less than six inches away from the American's face, and the buckshot nearly decapitated the man. The blond hair turned black as it mixed with blood, brains and other body fluids—the combined mess shooting in all directions.

For a moment, a shocked silence reined over the prairie. Before all hell broke loose.

Bolan dived behind the Wrangler, drawing the Desert Eagle as he hit the ground. A split second later he was on his knees, bracing the huge pistol on the Jeep's hood.

He spotted one of the preppies swinging an AK-47 his way. He ducked behind the Wrangler a microsecond before a rifle round sailed over the Jeep. He paused, knowing that if he could stay alive until the gunfight was over the Mexican and American drug dealers would do his work for him and kill each other off. There was a flaw in that plan, however. And it was a big one.

Lopez had taken him as far into the Jimenez organization as he could. The next step would require someone higher up the food chain. And that meant keeping Ricardo Sanchez alive.

Bolan rose from behind the Wrangler, his eyes scanning the area for Sanchez. But before he could spot the man he was again driven down behind the Jeep, this time by one of the Americans sputtering 9 mm rounds out of a HK MP-5. Moving low behind the vehicle's engine block, the Executioner leaned around the grille and brought the Desert Eagle up. A .44 Magnum shot from the Eagle's beak drilled through the nose of the preppie-clad submachine gunner.

Once more Bolan rose over the hood, searching for Sanchez. As his eyes scanned the prairie-turned-battlefield once more, he saw another of the preppies unload two rounds from a Remington pump gun into Frederico Lopez.

Bolan ducked again as a burst of fire from an M-16 flew

over the back of the Jeep. He could see other Jimenez men crouching behind their vehicles. With the Desert Eagle still in his right fist, Bolan curled his left hand back and under his jacket, grasping the grips of the Beretta 93-R. A moment later the machine pistol was turned toward the oncoming fire from the preppies, the long nose of the sound suppressor snaking up and over the back of the Wrangler. Flipping the selector to burst mode, the Executioner pulled the trigger.

An American drug dealer took the trio of near-silent 9 mm rounds squarely in the chest. Stumbling backward, he slammed into the Hummer and then slithered into a sitting position, his open eyes staring sightlessly for all eternity.

For a moment, the gunfire ceased. Bolan took advantage of the break in the bedlam to rise farther over the back of the Jeep to take in the situation. The Jimenez men had downed their share of the American, but they'd lost many men themselves. The bodies of Mexican drug runners littered the lighted area between the headlights of the Wrangler and Hummer.

As best the Executioner could make out, only three of Jimenez men were still alive. He could clearly see one man crouching behind the rear of the pickup, two more behind the Dodge. Just as he was about to turn his attention back to the fight he saw Sanchez's double-barreled shotgun appear over the trunk. Without even rising to see where he was shooting, Sanchez pointed the stumpy weapon in the general direction of the Hummer and Suburban and pulled one of the triggers, then the other.

The first of the spray-and-pray efforts struck the dirt three feet in front of the Hummer, killing nothing but grass and sandy soil. The second went wide of the Suburban.

The double-barreled shotgun disappeared to be reloaded.

It appeared that only three of the Americans were still alive. Two had taken refuge behind the Hummer. The third lurked somewhere out of sight near the Suburban.

Bolan moved to the front of the Jeep, leaned around the grille and surveyed the scene from that vantage point as auto-fire from behind the Hummer and Suburban resumed. A few of the rounds found their way to the Wrangler. But most seemed concentrated on the pickup, Dodge Dart and Camero. A dark cloud passed over the moon, and in the dim light it was hard to pinpoint the exact source of the gunfire. Suddenly the cloud moved on, and the Executioner saw the reflection of a preppie with a shaved head and goatee in the Suburban's rear window.

Quickly dropping the partially empty magazine in the Desert Eagle, Bolan slammed the one holding the armor-piercing rounds into the big gun. He aimed at the reflection in the glass and fired the hollowpoint round still in the chamber. The slug burst the glass of the rear window on the driver's side of the Suburban, flying on to shatter the image of the goateed face he'd seen in the reflection. But the bullet missed the preppie behind the Suburban, as he knew it would. The reflection had been distorted, telling the Executioner that it didn't betray the American's true location. He had fired the last hollowpoint round partially on the off chance that it would hit, but more to get rid of it, and chamber the first pointed full-metal bullets now in the weapon.

As the Mexicans continued to throw out sporadic fire from behind their vehicles, the Executioner lowered his point of aim to the rear door of the Suburban. He triggered off one round just below the door handle, then another roughly six inches below the first. Between the shattered windows, he saw pieces of upholstery and seat padding fly up into the air as the armor-piercing bullets drilled through the door on his side, then the seat, before exiting out of the other door.

If any death throes came from behind the Suburban, they went unheard. Before the explosions from the Desert Eagle had died down the Executioner shifted the front sight a foot to the right and fired twice more. He did the same to the left.

He kept his eyes on the Suburban as he ejected the super-penetrating rounds and jammed in a fresh magazine of hollowpoint rounds. He couldn't be sure that he'd hit the man behind the Suburban. But he didn't see him, or a weapon, rising up to return fire.

Turning his attention to the Hummer, Bolan saw a head move out to the side just in time to catch a bullet squarely between the eyes. A whoop of victory came from behind the pickup as the Executioner turned his attention to the final preppie firing from behind the Hummer's engine block. Not even the armor-piercing rounds were going to go through the Hummer, so he didn't bother changing magazines again. Instead, he lifted both the Desert Eagle and the Beretta and aimed at the spot where the man had last risen.

While the Mexicans continued to fill the air with explosions from their rifles and shotguns, Bolan waited. Finally, the man behind the Hummer rose until only the top of his head and eyes could be seen. The Executioner cut loose with a 3-round burst from the Beretta. The preppie slumped to his side on the ground.

But the Executioner knew his job was not yet over. Even though he had seen no movement behind the Suburban since he'd fired the armor-piercing rounds through the vehicle, he couldn't be certain that the American who had used it as cover was dead. Breaking into a sprint, he fired another 3-round burst from the 93-R and rounded the front of that vehicle.

He needn't have bothered. The American behind the Suburban had taken at least two rounds in the chest.

Bolan turned toward the Mexican drug runners who were beginning to rise from behind their vehicles. He had seen Sanchez's stubby-barreled scattergun behind the Camero. But that vehicle was the farthest from where Bolan stood. He meant to finish off the three Jimenez gunmen, then use Sanchez to take him higher in the organization. But if he shot the men now—and they were beginning to come out from hiding as he walked forward—Sanchez would have plenty of time to react and send a double-dose of buckshot his way.

Bolan met the trio of Mexican drug runners in the glow of the headlights between the Hummer and Wrangler. "You fight like *el diablo* himself," breathed one of the men. It was obvious that the Executioner's actions had proved to them that he was on their side.

Bolan didn't speak. He continued toward the Camero. As soon as he got close enough to Sanchez, he'd disarm the man. Then, before the others could take in what was really going on, he'd be done with them.

When the Executioner rounded the Camero, he did indeed see Ricardo Sanchez. But another Mexican drug runner was holding the sawed-off shotgun, and the leader of this Jimenez faction lay on his back, a lone hole in the center of his forehead.

Bolan stopped in his tracks.

"I'm in charge now," the man said as he brought up the double-barreled weapon.

For a moment, Bolan studied the glazed eyes of the man still crouched behind the Camero.

In a flash, Bolan brought up the Desert Eagle, pulled the trigger and split the man's head almost in two.

As the roar of the giant Magnum pistol filled the prairie, the Executioner lifted the Beretta in his other hand toward the three men in the headlights. Their awe at his combat prowess had suddenly turned to disbelief at what they had just seen. They took a moment before they could react.

Which gave Bolan the time he needed to dispatch them.

Still set for 3-round burst, the Executioner's first pull of the Beretta trigger splattered the face of the first. Before the man standing in the middle could react, another trio of quiet 9 mm hollow-point rounds ripped through the man's chest and tore his heart to pieces.

In his peripheral vision, Bolan could see the last man's arms begin to raise the AK-47 in his hands.

But he was still a half second too slow.

The Executioner's last tap of the trigger sent three more hollow-points coughing from the suppressor. The first two caught the Mexican gunman in the throat. The third round entered the drug runner's cheek just below the left eye and exited the side of his head, a trail of blood, bone and brains following it.

Finally, both the boom of the Desert Eagle and the hissing of the sound-suppressed Beretta died down. An eerie silence fell over the prairie.

It was only then that the Executioner was able to hear the soft moaning coming from just in front of the Dodge Dart.

Bolan turned both pistols that way, aiming them toward the sound. Just out of the direct beams of the headlights, he saw the shadowy form of a man. Lying on his back, his hands clutched his abdomen, trying to hold his intestines inside.

Holstering the Desert Eagle, Bolan kept one eye and an ear cocked for signs that any of the other Mexicans or Americans might still be alive. The Beretta still at the ready, he dropped to one knee next to the man.

"Father...forgive me," the agonized voice whispered.

"I'm not a priest," the Executioner said. "I'm not the one you need to ask for forgiveness."

The dying man nodded. "I have sinned," he whispered around the blood that was almost choking him.

"We all have," said the Executioner. "What's your name?"

"Jorge," the man breathed. "Am I dying?"

Bolan looked at the man's wounds. If they'd been across the street from a hospital emergency room, with a team of skilled surgeons there and ready, Jorge might have had a small glimmer of hope. But Reynosa was the closest city, and they were at least thirty miles away. There was no way the Executioner could get the man to a hospital in time to save his life.

"Yes," Bolan said, "you are."

The dying man broke into tears.

"You're dying and, like you said, you've sinned," the Executioner said. "But here, at the very end of your life, you've got one last chance to do something good."

The man's eyes looked met Bolan's. "What?" he asked as blood dribbled from his lips. "Tell me what I can do."

"Tell me all you can about the Jimenez operation," the Executioner said. "Tell me about this deal that's supposed to go down soon with the hi-tech weaponry."

"I have...only heard...this rumor," Jorge said. "Sanchez knew about it, I think. He said it would change the way the arrogant *norteamericanos* live forever."

Bolan could see the man's eyes starting to glaze over; his life was draining fast. "Tell me anything else you know," he said. "I'm going all the way to the top on this thing. All the way to Jimenez himself."

For a moment, the cloudy eyes became sharp again. Jorge said, "There is another rumor...." His voice trailed off and his eyes closed.

For a moment the Executioner thought he was dead. Reaching out, he grasped the man by the shoulder and gently shook him. "Jorge," he said. "This other rumor? What is it?"

Jorge gasped, "Jimenez is *not* the top man." He panted hard with each word. "He is...only a front for..."

The Executioner shook his head, frowning. "What do you mean, Jorge?" he asked. "Who's the real man at the top? Who's actually behind the Jimenez organization?"

The Mexican's eyes had taken on a glassy stare, but he could still hear. "I don't...know," he breathed in an ever-weakening voice. "But he is...someone well-known. Someone...famous."

Bolan's frown deepened. "Mexican or American?" he asked.

Jorge's head moved slowly back and forth. He didn't know. His chest stopped moving up and down.

Bolan stood and surveyed the dead bodies around him in the headlights of the Hummer and Wrangler. Ricardo Sanchez was among the dead, which meant there would be no using him to move higher up the chain of command within the Jimenez organization.

Bolan would have to create his own inroad into the organization. He would be on his own.

There was nothing new about that.

2

From the passenger's seat, Chad Kauffman pretended to talk to the driver of the Chrysler as the black-and-white patrol car passed. But, even as his lips moved, he kept his eyes glued to the two uniformed men in the front seat. They were chatting amiably as well, and took no notice of the Chrysler.

Of course there was no reason they should, Kauffman thought, as he watched the police car fade out of sight over a rise in the street several blocks past the bank. From the waist up, he looked little different than any of the local farmers who had changed out of their daily overalls into a more dressy look for a trip into town. Atop his head was a straw cowboy hat carefully shaped into the most conservative of Western styles. His chest and shoulders were covered by an equally drab Western shirt.

Besides, Kauffman thought, he and his crew had stolen the Chrysler from a farmhouse just outside of town less than thirty minutes earlier. And by the time they'd departed there had been no one left on the farm who was in any shape to use a telephone.

Kauffman glanced toward the woman behind the wheel as

he removed his hat long enough to wrap the walkie-talkie headset over his ears. Sheila Brown wore a white blouse that accented her topaz skin. Kauffman knew that a black woman riding with a white man in Kingfisher, Oklahoma, might raise a few eyebrows. But his driver was light enough to pass as a Latina, and that was a common enough sight. The scarf Sheila wore tied beneath her chin concealed her face.

Kauffman knew they had drawn no unwanted attention. Because, like he did before all bank jobs, he had done his homework, researching not only the bank itself but the Kingfisher, Oklahoma, community around it.

"How long?" Brown asked as Kauffman replaced the straw hat on his head.

"Two minutes," he said. Twisting in his seat, he scanned up and down the street but saw no further signs of police. They had been parked on Kingfisher's main street for nearly five minutes, and none of the shoppers going in and out of the storefronts seemed to have noticed them. That's what made a town like Kingfisher a perfect target. It was small enough to lack top-notch law enforcement, but large enough that not everyone knew one another, or paid much attention to new faces going about their business.

The top of Kauffman's dark green coveralls had been folded down at the waist, and now he lifted them up and slid his arms into the sleeves. He knew he would still fit in with the scenery. With a local economy depending on agriculture and oil, it was not unusual to see a farmer or oil-field rough-neck dressed as he was—even in the heat.

Buckling the pistol belt around his waist beneath the window, Kauffman plugged the headset into the receiver attached opposite his gun and tapped the transmit button. "Liberation One to Liberation Two," he spoke into the mouthpiece.

"L-Two, still in position," came the gruff voice of Delbert Washington, his second in command. Dressed similarly to Kauffman, Washington's Chevrolet pickup—also appropriated from the elderly farm couple who would no longer need it—was parked near the other end of Kingfisher's main street. When Brown had driven them past a few minutes earlier, both the black man riding shotgun and his white driver, Ansel Reynolds, had been slurping ICEEs through straws.

"Affirmative," Kauffman said. "Stand by." He paused, licking his lips. As always, his mouth and throat had turned dry as the moment of truth neared. But the adrenaline rush surging through his body more than made up for the slight discomfort, and it was a dryness he had learned to look forward to.

Preparing to rob a bank—or carry out any of the other dangerous missions he and his crew took on—provided him with a high he experienced in no other way. Not with grass, not with coke—not even with heroin or LSD. Adrenaline, he had decided, was his drug of choice. And the fact that he could put it to good use for humanity was just icing on the cake. Kauffman glanced quickly toward Brown. Not even in the throes of sex with a passionate woman like her gave him the kind of high he was experiencing.

"L-One to L-Three," Kauffman said into the mic.

"L-Three," a voice on the other end responded. The transmission was slightly scratchy so Kauffman adjusted the squelch. "Just passing the courthouse again," Micah Strong said.

Kauffman smiled—a rare occurrence, and enough to make his driver turn toward him. Brown's eyebrows lowered slightly beneath the scarf, and it was clear she was wondering if something was wrong. To relieve her concern, Kauffman shook his head nonchalantly. But inwardly, he felt a wave of pride mix with the adrenaline high still shooting through him.

Chad Kauffman, III, knew he was not like other men. He was stern. Stern enough that—at least to those who knew him—a smile was interpreted the opposite of the way it was in other men. And the other members of his core group had told him more than once that when the action began—action such as robbing a bank, or interrogating someone suspected of being a traitor to the cause—a truly frightening smile came to his face.

"Situation report," Kauffman said into the mic.

"All but one city police vehicle is still here," Strong came back. "We just passed the other one heading out of town."

"And the sheriff?" Kauffman asked.

"His car's still here. Three deputy cars gone. But we haven't seen any of them inside the city limits so they're most likely out in the county somewhere."

"Affirmative," Kauffman said. "Stay prepared in case any of that changes."

"That's a 10-4," came the answer from the third vehicle.

Kauffman looked down at his watch once more and saw that they had less than thirty seconds before they began. He thought briefly of Strong and the other three men in the car he referred to as the "rover." The vehicle was a Cadillac. But unlike the pickup and Chrysler, it had not come from the home of the dead farm couple. They had boosted it the day before in an affluent residential area of Oklahoma City, and along with the Dodge van that was now stashed in the farm couple's barn, it had brought them to Kingfisher that morning. It was not likely to have been reported stolen yet, either.

A dead yuppie and his wife, decaying on the expensive carpet in their living room, could attest to that.

"Fifteen seconds," Kauffman said into the mic. "Get ready." He watched the second hand on the face of his wristwatch, then began his countdown. "Ten...nine...eight," he said into the microphone in front of his face, proceeding down to one and then ending the transmission with, "Go."

Brown backed out of the parking space and started toward the bank. Down the street, Kauffman could see Reynolds and Washington heading toward them. The two vehicles turned into opposite ends of the bank's parking lot at the same time.

Brown and Reynolds knew their jobs well, and came to a halt directly in front of the bank's main entrance. Kauffman tossed his straw cowboy hat over the seat and jerked a stocking cap from one of the pockets of his coveralls. From the floorboard at his feet, he lifted a brown leather briefcase.

After Kauffman got out of the Chrysler, Brown began backing into one of the handicapped parking places.

Delbert Washington, in his own coveralls and carrying a similar briefcase, met Kauffman ten feet from the front doors as Reynolds backed into another of the handicapped spaces. The black man lifted a hand to his face, scratching his forehead as Kauffman turned his back to the entrance. Walking sideways, his face never in view of the surveillance camera and Washington's covered by his scratching hand, the two men appeared to be locked in conversation as they entered the breezeway that led into the bank proper. But as the glass door swung shut behind them, the two men suddenly gave up the facade.

The breezeway was a blind spot in the bank's security surveillance. Kauffman knew that from the scouting expedition he'd done the day before. One camera covered the outside of the building, but the next one wouldn't pick them up until they burst through the next set of doors. Donning their stocking caps and pulling the face masks down over their chins, Kauffman and Washington yanked their matching HK MP-5 submachine guns from their briefcases as they opened the doors.

Kauffman dropped his briefcase at his feet and fired a burst of 9 mm bullets into the two surveillance cameras he'd spotted the day before. The explosions not only ended the video-taping, they served to get the attention of both bank employees and patrons.

Shrieks and howls of fear went up from the men and women around the bank until Kauffman fired another burst into the ceiling. It had always struck him as funny how the first shots he fired started the screaming but the next always ended it.

He launched into his opening speech. "Greetings, ladies and gentlemen, employees and customers, of the First National Bank of Kingfisher, Oklahoma. Your enslavement to free enterprise and the imperialistic government that holds you in bondage is about to be partially diminished. The New

Symbionese Liberation Army regrets that it cannot, at this time, eradicate U.S. commercialism in its entirety. But such freedom is coming."

Kauffman paused for a moment, waiting. This was the point when would-be heroes—if there were any—would make their move. This time there was one. And he did.

The wrinkled, clawlike fingers of a uniformed guard, seventy years old if he was a day, suddenly fumbled for the revolver on his hip. Washington didn't hesitate. Twisting at the waist, Kauffman's second in command held the trigger back on his MP-5 and sent a steady stream of fire into the old man, making him jerk back and forth like the marionette of a crazed puppeteer.

The guard slumped to the floor in a pool of crimson as more screams echoed through the bank lobby. Kauffman swept his MP-5 in an arc, firing another long stream just above head level.

"Please lay facedown on the floor," he said when the roar of the rounds had died down. His words were unnecessary. Except for Washington and himself, everyone had their faces pressed against the tile, their hands covering their heads.

Two women, who appeared to be loan officers, sat frozen at their desks just to Kauffman's side. He waved his MP-5 and they nearly dived out of their chairs, joining the others on the floor.

Washington pushed quickly through the door to the rear of the tellers' windows. A second later, he had crowded four frightened women and a young man into one of the cages. All five faces stared in horror at Kauffman's masked face as he said in a calm voice, "So. Who knows the combination to the safe?"

The faces continued to stare, silent.

Another burst brought an incoherent babble from the quintet.

"You," Kauffman said. "Young man. What's your name?"

The boy opened his mouth. "Andy," he said. His voice had the tenor of a frightened little girl, and brought a loud guffaw from Washington.

"Well, Andy," Kauffman said. "Do you know the combination of the safe?"

The terrified youth shook his head back and forth.

"I think Andy's a liar, Pentad," Washington said, speaking for the first time.

"It would appear that he is," Kauffman concurred. "Take him to the safe. If he hasn't learned the combination by the time you get there, kill him."

The statement forced words from the mouth of a middle-aged woman with frosted hair. "He doesn't know it," she said in a trembling voice. "I do."

Kauffman lifted his left hand from the foregrip of his weapon and waved toward the back of the bank. "If you would be so kind, then…" he said, letting his voice trail off pleasantly. As Washington followed the woman out of sight, he ordered the other women and Andy to place their hands on the counter where he could see them. Then, with a final warning to the people on the floor not to move, he grabbed up the briefcase he'd dropped next to him and hurried through the door to the tellers' windows himself.

Glancing at his watch, he saw that just under forty-five seconds had elapsed.

Shoving the briefcase into the hands of the frightened young man, Kauffman forced him along the row of teller's windows, emptying the cash registers. When they had reached the end, Kauffman shoved the youth back through the door to the lobby. A second later, Washington appeared with his briefcase overflowing and a second cloth bag stuffed with bills. "Too much to carry it all," he shouted as he followed the woman with the frosted hair through the door. "But I got all the hundreds."

Kauffman nodded as he checked his watch again. They were nearing their ninety-second maximum allotted time. It was time to go, not get greedy and make more trips. There was no way of knowing if any of the bank personnel had tripped a silent alarm. Banks were getting more creative these days, and no longer relied on buttons hidden beneath the tellers' windows. Kauffman knew any number of seemingly innocent movements could have notified the police of the robbery in progress.

"Then let us bid these fine people adieu," Kauffman said. He motioned Washington forward. His second in command raised his MP-5, brought the barrel down on top of the frosted hair in front of him, and stepped over the woman as she crumpled to the tiles.

"It would be ill-mannered of me not to warn you that this bank was wired with plastic explosives last night while all of you were sleeping," Kauffman said as they prepared to leave. "The explosion will level the building, and can be detonated by a remote control in the hands of more of our personnel who will be monitoring this site for the next fifteen minutes." The statement, of course, was preposterous. But experience had taught Kauffman that, at this point, the terrified people on the floor were ready to believe anything. "If any attempt is made to contact the authorities before then…well, you get the picture, don't you?"

A variety of murmurs of understanding met his ears. But just by chance, Kauffman realized that the young male teller named Andy—now on the floor facedown at his feet—had not responded. Gently nudging the youth's shoulder with the toe of his boot, he said, "You. Andy. Do you understand?"

But fear had frozen the young man's voice and limbs.

"I suppose I must take your failure to respond as a 'no,' Andy," Kauffman said. Then, pressing the barrel of the MP-5 against the back of the boy's head, he pulled the trigger and let three rounds send blood and body parts shooting through the air.

The adrenaline rush was incredible.

Kauffman and Washington had five seconds to spare on their ninety-second maximum exposure time when they got back into their vehicles. Brown and Reynolds pulled their vehicles out of the parking lot with no more urgency than they would if their passengers had just made a deposit. The two vehicles were a block away from the bank before they heard the first siren.

Kauffman tapped the microphone still in front of his face and said, "L-One to L-Three. Come in, Three."

"Three hears you," Strong said.

"Any problems?" Kauffman asked.

"Not if you're already on the road," Strong replied. "We

just passed the courthouse again and they're all headed your way. You should see them in a few seconds."

As they passed the spot where Washington had waited earlier, they met the first of six city police and county sheriff's vehicles tearing down the street toward the bank.

Kauffman had his cowboy hat back on and his coveralls pulled down to his waist to expose his Western shirt. They blended into the other traffic so well that as they passed the flashing red and blue lights, he was almost tempted to wave.

Suppressing the desire, Kauffman instead reached into a pocket of his coveralls and pulled out a remote-control device much like the fictitious one he'd described to the terrified men and women on the floor of the bank. He remembered his lie about wiring the building.

He had done some wiring, all right. But not at the bank.

Looking at the device in his hands, Kauffman thought about how much it resembled a simple television remote control. The primary difference was that there were no buttons to change channels or volume. Instead, the face of the remote sported only a series of numbers one through nine. Kauffman smiled. Nine was more than he'd needed anyway.

Kauffman began to tap the numerals. As he did, he heard a series of explosions behind him. Looking into the side mirror, he saw flames and smoke rising from various points in downtown Kingfisher.

The explosive wiring Washington had done the night before had been beneath the vehicles belonging to the police and sheriff's department. It had been too easy. The rubes wearing their tin stars and ten-gallon cowboy hats left the cars completely unattended, either in front of their houses or outside the courthouse, every night.

As they passed the city limits and headed out onto Oklahoma State Highway 81, Kauffman pushed the final button. Another explosion rose up from the area of the Kingfisher County courthouse. That would have been the car driven by the sheriff himself.

Fifteen minutes later Brown and the others turned onto a dirt road. Following a gravel path past the farmhouse, they stopped in front of the barn. The Cadillac was in the lead, and Micah Strong's burly form got out of the passenger's seat and slid the splintered barn door open. All three vehicles pulled inside.

Five minutes later they were back in the Dodge van and pulling away from the farmhouse.

"HOW MUCH DID WE GET?" Delbert Washington asked as he pulled a tightly rolled marijuana cigarette from the breast pocket of his Western shirt.

Kauffman had just finished counting the cash. He settled back in the seat behind Strong who was driving. "A little over three hundred thousand," he said.

"Not bad, Field Marshal Pentad," Brown said, hugging his arm.

"No," Kauffman said. "Not bad at all." But in his mind, he knew it was not enough. Not *nearly* enough to pay for the special shipment he was about to receive from his contact in Mexico. He would have to come up with some way of making a lot more money than he was getting from these bank robberies and the drugs that other members of the NSLA were selling around the country. And he didn't have much time to do it, either.

Brown threw both arms around Kauffman, and he felt the urgency in her hug. He knew he was in for a hot time as soon as they were far enough away from Kingfisher to be out of danger. He grinned. He was not the only one to experience a high from robbers and other violence. Such actions always got his woman's blood pressure rising, too.

The other members of the NSLA core group had no need to know that they were still short of money, so Kauffman said, "It's enough to keep us going for a while. Let the Revolution continue."

"Let the Revolution continue," the other members of the New Symbionese Liberation Army shouted in unison, raising their right fists at the same time.

Chad Kauffman settled back against his seat, closed his eyes and smiled.

Sheila Brown was already unzipping his pants.

3

While Jorge was dying, the Executioner had stayed ready with the Beretta in case any of the other dead bodies came back to life. More than once in his long career, a man who had appeared to have breathed his last breath had suddenly found enough life left in him for one last pull of the trigger.

Satisfied that Jorge was gone for good, Bolan rose to his feet. Quickly, he made the rounds of the bodies scattered between the vehicles, pressing a thumb and middle finger into the carotid arteries of each man to check for a pulse. He found none.

When the last body had been checked Bolan circled through the various vehicles, adding the headlights of the other cars and trucks to the illumination afforded by the Wrangler and Hummer. When he was finished, he had almost as much light to work with as he'd have had at high noon. Slowly and more methodically, he began to search the bodies again, this time for any clues that might lead him toward Jimenez and whoever the mystery man was who really headed the Jimenez organization.

Bolan knew if he was going to bring down the Mexican crime syndicate before the high-tech weapons smuggling deal went down, he needed a new story, a new lead. He was hoping to find it on the bodies of the men who had brought the cocaine.

The Executioner was sorely disappointed.

When he had searched all of the Jimenez men and found nothing of value, he turned his attention to the Americans. They were decked out in the latest fraternity boy fashions and Bolan had suspected the outfits were rather naive attempt to mislead U.S. Customs officials when they crossed back over the border with the drugs. Looking closer, Bolan saw that most of the Americans were indeed of college age. A few appeared to be in their late twenties, and a couple had already seen the better side of thirty.

Frowning, the Executioner stared down at the white pasty face of a man in his early twenties. Could they really *be* college students? he wondered. Even in death, their faces lacked the toughened look of the career criminal. Bolan knew that regardless of which side of the law they were on, hard men lived hard lives, and their faces began to reflect it early in life. He concluded that these young men had only recently turned to crime.

And paid the price for not being very good at it.

As he had already done with the Jimenez men, Bolan searched the pockets of the dead Americans. As with the Mexicans, he found no forms of identification whatsoever. That didn't surprise him. Men heading out to do an illegal act by the light of the moon rarely carried anything that would directly lead authorities back to their identities. The Jimenez men would simply have left their identification at home. But the Americans would have known that some form of identification might be required to cross the border. So either genuine or phony, they would have brought passports, driver's licences, voter's registration cards, or *something* that proved they were U.S. citizens.

So where were those forms of identification?

Bolan began a methodical search of the Hummer and Suburban in which the Americans had arrived. Not only did the two vehicles reveal no clue as to the identities of their passengers, the registrations, insurance, and all other identifying papers had been removed as well.

For a moment Bolan stood in the midst of the intersecting headlights and stared up at the starlit sky. Both the Suburban and Hummer had Texas tags, which meant they'd been driven across the border. The secret to who these men were had to be hidden somewhere, either on them, or in the vehicles themselves.

Bolan knew the next step in the search of the vehicles would be to completely strip them down to parts. But, somehow, he didn't think that was where the key to the Americans' identities lay.

Bolan recalled a tiny discrepancy he had noticed earlier. While all of the Americans had been dressed in the latest "frat rat" styles, the sandy-haired leader had worn a belt at least twice as wide as the others.

Returning to where the American leader had fallen, Bolan made another quick search of his pockets. Again finding nothing, he unbuckled the man's belt and slid it through the loops. Running a hand down the length of the strip of leather, he searched for a zipper, but found none. So much for his theory that the sandy-haired man had worn a money belt containing a clue to the location of the missing identification.

The Executioner was about to drop the belt when another idea hit him. Dropping back to his knees, he unzipped the man's zipper and pulled his khaki slacks just below the waist

There, by the light of the moon and the headlights, he saw a small lump in the American's white briefs. Held in place by the underwear's elastic waistband, it was positioned to fit just under the wide belt.

Bolan reached into the waistband. His hand came out holding a small key with a plastic grip.

Rising, the Executioner leaned down and held the key in front of the Hummer's headlight beam. It was a locker key of some kind, the type found in airports, train stations and bus terminals all over the world. In the brighter light he could see the number embossed on the green plastic grip: 307.

Bolan stared at the key. He might not have found all he'd have liked to find on the dead men, but he suspected he'd found all he was going to.

Pocketing the key, Bolan moved quickly.

WITH MONEY TO FINANCE the rest of his campaign against the Jimenez syndicate in the back seat, Bolan started the engine, threw the Jeep into first and took off down the same grassy path he and Lopez had come in on. He had just reached the highway linking Reynosa to Monterrey when he heard the Hummer explode.

Looking back as he made the turn onto the broken concrete, he saw a ball of fire rising toward the heavens. A second later another explosion, smaller than the first, also illuminated the night sky as the pickup went up.

And somewhere between the two vehicles, the white powder that had been about to enter the United States met an equally fiery demise.

Bolan gripped the locker key in his left fist as he used his right to shift through the Wrangler's gears. He couldn't be sure but his instincts told him the key in his hand would lead to the identities of the Americans. And an even deeper hunch made him wonder if they weren't somehow involved in the high-tech weapons deal about to go down.

The Executioner's jaw locked tight as he sped on through the night, back toward Reynosa. The first thing to do, was find out exactly what story this simple locker key had to tell.

Reynosa, Mexico, was little different than the dozens of other border towns stretching from the Gulf of Mexico to the Pacific Ocean. It had been founded across from McAllen, Texas, during the nineteenth century and from its very beginning the chief industries had been tourism and smuggling.

Bolan reached the sleepy outskirts of the city a little before one in the morning. He thought about money in the briefcase just behind him in the Wrangler, and wished for a moment that there was some way he could distribute it throughout the poverty he saw before him. Just beyond Reynosa's booming inner city—where the rich got richer—the poor got poorer.

But short of stopping and handing out the money on the street, the Executioner saw no way to solve the problem. Besides, to do so would only temporarily alleviate the poverty. What was needed was not a Band-Aid solution but a *cure*. And part of that cure would be using the money to put an end to organizations such as the Jimenez syndicate, which victimized the poor.

As he neared the center of town, the lights brightened and noise picked up. Traffic slowed, and he found himself caught in what seemed like an endless line of red traffic lights. Bolan took advantage of the break in the action to go back over his earlier train of thought.

He was playing a hunch, he knew, but it was the best thing he had to go on at the moment. His gut-level instincts told him the key would open a locker at the Reynosa bus station.

Bolan knew he could be wrong, but he doubted the Americans had driven on to Monterrey during their visit. They'd have stashed their IDs somewhere safe, convenient and accessible between the border and the isolated spot where the deal had been set to go down. That meant Reynosa.

The soldier knew Reynosa's small airport would be likely to have lockers like the bus station. So would the train depot, which sent its ancient locomotives chugging deeper into the country. But both were several miles out of the way, and he remembered passing the bus station with Lopez when they'd driven through the city earlier in the day.

Bolan was well into the nightlife area of the city by the time he spotted the bus station again. Bars, brothels, gambling halls and other entertainment enterprises that depended on Mexico's more lucrative neighbor to the north were in full swing. Provocatively dressed women stood on every street corner, and men standing outside the establishments did their best to lure pedestrians inside with all of the enthusiasm of carnival barkers. The sidewalks were filled with as many American men as Mexicans. Many looked like the South Texas college boys the dealers he'd taken out had appeared to be, while other young men with short hair and erect postures might as well have had "U.S. serviceman" stamped on their foreheads.

But regardless of where they had come from, the young Americans were all there for the same reasons: cheap souvenirs, cheap booze and cheap women.

Spotting an open parking spot along the street, the Executioner pulled the Wrangler over. He had barely killed the engine and reached behind him for the briefcase full of drug money when he was descended upon by an army of street urchins. None could have been over ten years old, yet all had the weary faces of children who were undernourished, undereducated and unsupervised. Bolan knew from experience that many of their fathers were in the cheaper cantinas in other parts of the city while their mothers plied their trade on the streets or in the brothels.

A lad with unkempt black hair almost covering his eyes stepped forward. "We guard your car," he said. "Just little *dinero.*"

Bolan smiled at the young entrepreneur. Such boys were present in every Mexican border town. He knew that "we guard your car" actually meant was that the eight young men he saw before him wouldn't steal the hubcaps and everything else they could carry off, or call their older brothers to come get the whole vehicle, if he paid them.

Reaching into his pocket, Bolan pulled out a roll of bills. Careful to keep the size of the roll and the larger denominations hidden from the young eyes below his hands, he counted off nine one-dollar bills and gave one each to the leader's accomplices. The young man who had spoken got two. He looked sadly at the boys again, wishing he could do more. But giving them too much money would be worse than none at all. They'd mark him down as a rich stupid gringo and then would certainly call their older brothers and fathers to try to roll him when he came out of the bus station.

And the Executioner had a mission. A mission that didn't allow for a time out while he battled common street thieves.

Briefcase in hand, Bolan crossed the grimy parking lot to the bus station. Through the greasy glass window he could see the rows of lockers even before he got to the door. As he moved through the waiting area, he passed more decrepit men, women and children who sat waiting for the buses that would take them back to their home villages. Among them, and seemingly oblivious to the way they stood out from the rest of the crowd, was a young American couple dressed in the finest traveling gear L.L. Bean had to offer.

The Executioner shook his head as he walked toward the lockers. He found 307 quickly and held his breath as he inserted the key, knowing that if he'd been wrong he'd be further delayed checking out the airport and train station. Even then, he might find that the key led him nowhere and that would mean he was back to ground zero.

The Executioner let the air out of his lungs again as the key twisted and the locker door popped open.

Inside, Bolan saw the stack of billfolds and two large envelopes. The envelopes, he suspected, would contain the registrations and other papers missing from the Hummer and Suburban. But this was no place to start checking out such details.

After a quick glance around to make sure no one was watching, Bolan opened the top of the briefcase and shoveled the entire contents of the locker inside on top of the drug money. He closed the door in front of him, and five seconds later was back on the street.

"Hombre!" a loud voice called out to his side.

Bolan turned to see an overweight Mexican wearing soiled green pants and a straw hat. A well-chewed toothpick extended from his teeth. "What you want, amigo?" the man asked as he stopped next to Bolan. "You want woman? I got woman."

The Executioner shook his head and started to turn away, but the man grabbed him by the sleeve.

Bolan turned around and something in his eyes caused the Mexican to drop his hand. "Drugs?" he said. "I got smack, coke, marijuana. You want roofies, amigo? I got roofies."

Again, Bolan shook his head.

The fat man moved in closer and in a conspiratorial way said, "Paco knows what you want. You want young boy, eh? I got young boy for you."

Bolan knew he didn't have time to get involved in Reynosa's street crime. But he *did* have time to backhand the fat man offering him the young boy, and knock out several of his teeth.

So he did.

As the man lay moaning on the sidewalk, Bolan started toward the Wrangler again. But as he neared it, he saw a narrow set of steps leading upward just to the side of a bar. Music blared from the open door of the tavern as a young serviceman exited and started up the steps with an overly made up woman with smooth brown skin. Bolan saw the sign above the steps read Hotel. It was obviously a place where the prostitutes took their tricks after picking them up in the bar next door.

The Executioner didn't want a prostitute. But a private room where he could go over the contents of the bus station locker was *exactly* what he needed.

The young American and his date for the night were disappearing down a hall when Bolan arrived at the check-in desk at the top of the stairs. "You want a woman?" the clerk asked him. The man obviously had his own stable for anyone who didn't want to bother going into the bar next door.

Bolan shook his head. "Just a place to sleep," he said.

The man behind the counter nodded and said, "Five dollars U.S.," and took a key from one of the hooks on the wall behind him.

Two minutes later the Executioner had dumped the money, wallets and registration papers on the worn bedspread of his room. He sat down to go through them.

Next door, through the thin wall, it sounded as if the guy from the bar who'd preceded him up the steps was getting his money's worth.

4

Bolan stared at the contents of the various wallets spread across the frayed bedspread as he lifted the ancient black rotary phone on the nightstand. Dialing the number to Stony Man Farm, he listened to a series of clicks and dial tones as the call was automatically routed through six different countries on three continents before finally reaching its final destination. This process, he knew, would defeat even the most high-tech tracing devices should anyone happen to be onto him or anyone else working out of the Farm.

With all of Stony Man's other security precautions in place, this was all but impossible. But the Executioner had seen the long shot come through during his career, and he knew that every step taken toward secrecy was another step toward life rather than death.

Finally, the line connected. As Bolan heard the receiver being lifted, he knew the automatic scrambling system would come on, turning the conversation at both ends into babble for any curious outside ears. "Hello, Striker," Barbara Price said, using the Executioner's mission code name.

"Hi," Bolan said, picturing the beautiful blond mission controller.

"I need the Bear."

"Hang on," Price said just as simply, and Bolan heard another click over the line.

A moment later, Aaron "The Bear" Kurtzman picked up his extension. "Long time no see," Kurtzman said. "Where are you, Striker?"

"Reynosa, Mexico," Bolan replied. "But I need to be in Miami."

"I'll contact Jack Grimaldi and get a plane started—"

"That's not what I meant," Bolan said, interrupting. "I just need it to *appear* that I'm in Miami on someone's caller ID." He took a deep breath. "But I'm getting ahead of myself, Bear. First, I need you to run down some names for me. I've got driver's licenses, passports, voter registrations and Social Security cards. They look good, but they could all just be good fakes."

"What makes you say that?" Kurtzman asked.

"Some of them look like they just came off the printing press," Bolan came back. "The rest look like they've been artificially aged. One of the voter's registration cards has been folded back and forth and crumpled. But the paper in between the creases is new. The corners of one of the driver's licenses are brown and slightly curled, telling me that somebody tried that old trick of sticking it in the oven for a while. Some of the other documents were soaked in water. Want me to go on?"

"Nope," Kurtzman said. "Sounds like you're right. Just read me the names and numbers and I'll verify your suspicions."

Bolan did, listening to Kurtzman's fingers tapping the information onto his computer keyboard as he spoke. The whole process took less than five minutes, and Kurtzman had the results almost instantly.

"Just as you thought, every last identity you gave me is false," Kurtzman confirmed.

Looking down at the registration papers for the Hummer and Suburban that had been crammed into the bus station locker with the wallets, the Executioner read that information off as well.

"I'm sure this won't surprise you, either," the computer whiz said a few seconds later. "But those two vehicles don't exist."

"The men who died around them will be happy to hear that," Bolan said. "Okay. What we've got here is an organization with contacts to some great document forgers. But I still don't know who they are, so let's jump on to the next thing I need."

"The part about where you're in Miami without really being in Miami," Kurtzman said.

"Right. I'm getting ready to make a call to Mexico City. To the Fernando Jimenez residence. Their caller ID needs to show me in Florida."

"Mere child's play," Kurtzman said. "Give me the number you're calling from in Reynosa."

Bolan looked at the faded white circle in the middle of the rotary phone, then read off the area code and number. He heard Kurtzman typing again, then another series of clicks sounded on the line. The noise ended with a short buzzing sound and then a beep, and then Kurtzman said, "Done, big fella. Your area code will show up as 305—Miami, Florida." The man in the wheelchair paused for a moment, then went on. "Want this set up so it'll ring you there in Reynosa if they want to call back?"

Bolan thought for a moment, then said, "No. On second thought, I need to come back to the Farm and pick up a few things. So I guess you ought to have Barb get Jack started this way with the plane after all. But tell him he can take his time. It's been a good three days since I've closed my eyes, and if I don't get an hour or two of sleep I'm going to fall off my feet."

"So what else is new?" Kurtzman said. "Jack just got back from bringing Phoenix Force in from the Rwanda job. He'll need to refuel and go through a routine maintenance check anyway. The timing ought to work out about right." There was a short pause, then the computer genius said, "Hang on while I tell Barb to advise him." The Executioner heard yet another click in his ear as he went on hold.

As he waited, the Executioner's thoughts turned to Jack Grimaldi, Stony Man Farm's top pilot. Years ago, Grimaldi had worked for the Mafia, flying some of the Mob's top crime bosses all over the world. But Bolan had brought out the good in the man, and Grimaldi had turned over a new leaf. Since that time, they had worked countless missions together, and there was no man in the world the Executioner trusted more.

Kurtzman came back on the line. "Didn't see any sense in wasting time. Jack's fueling up even as we speak."

"Great," Bolan said. "As far as the callback line goes, let's just hook the Jimenez bunch into one of the Farm's lines. Tell Barb to answer it with 'Mikhailovich Imports' if it rings."

"And what might Mikhailovich Imports be?" Kurtzman asked.

"My front," Bolan said. "I'm about to become Anton Mikhailovich, Russian immigrant entrepreneur who imports a lot more than just the caviar he advertises."

"And my guess is that you'd like some help making this Mikhailovich come to life," Kurtzman said.

"Jimenez and his group have Mexican police connections so they'll be able to check up on me," Bolan said. "I'll need a phony criminal record inserted into the Russian *militsia* files. Let's give me a couple of drug-trafficking arrests and a manslaughter charge. But no convictions." Bolan didn't want to risk being asked specific questions about prison. He knew nothing could blow a cover faster than that.

As Kurtzman's fingers tapped away at his keyboard, the computer man said, "You want any record here in the U.S.?"

"No," Bolan said. "That's why I immigrated. I'm looking for a clean start. But have Hal insert a couple of intelligence reports into the Justice Department files. Make them suspicious of my import business. And add some similar intel to Interpol."

"Consider it done, Striker," Kurtzman said.

"Thanks, Bear."

"Anything else?" Kurtzman asked.

"Not on this end," the Executioner said. "Anything happening back there?"

"Same old same old," Kurtzman said. "That pair of bank

robbers and their drivers are still hitting the Southwest. They even blew up the responding police vehicles in a little town called Kingfisher, Oklahoma. Must have wired the cars the night before."

Bolan nodded. He remembered hearing about the robberies just before leaving for a quick job in Thailand before he'd entered Mexico with Lopez. The robberies had gone down like clockwork with only two things making them stand out: First had been the unnecessary violence. In addition to the exploding vehicles Kurtzman had just mentioned, several bank employees and customers had been murdered for no apparent reason other than the robbers liked it. And second, the two men who actually entered the banks had shouted a lot of political hogwash throughout the events. Local law-enforcement officers figured it was done simply to mislead them.

"Okay," Bolan said. "I'm going to call Jimenez, then catch a few z's. What's Jack's status now?"

"Flyboy will be taking off within the hour."

"Great. Tell him I'll be waiting for him at the airport when he gets here."

"Good luck," Kurtzman said. "See you when you get in."

Bolan looked at his watch and saw it was almost three a.m., hardly the right time for the type of call he was about to make. He dropped the telephone receiver into its cradle.

Scooping the wallets and their scattered contents off the bedspread and dropping them back into the briefcase, the Executioner walked to the door and checked the lock. The light switch was next to the door and he flipped it down. Suddenly, the room took on an eerie semidarkness illuminated by a strange rainbow of colors coming in around the window blinds from the neon signs on the street. Bolan walked back to the bed. He could still hear the music from the bars and the occasional shout from a drunk. Next door to his room, it sounded as if the American who had preceded him up the stairs with the prostitute had paid for a second round.

Shrugging out of the Beretta's shoulder harness and sliding the Desert Eagle and TOPS SAW knife off his belt, the Executioner dropped his weapons on the side of the bed where the wallets had been before.

Both weapons needed a good cleaning, but he didn't have the right solvents and other equipment with him, and he could turn them over to John "Cowboy" Kissinger, Stony Man Farm's chief armorer, when he arrived at the Farm the next day.

Jerking the sound-suppressed Beretta out of its holster, Bolan dropped to his back on the other side of the bed. Experience had taught him that when the opportunity for a few hours of sleep presented itself he should take advantage of it. Once a mission began, another such opportunity might not arrive for days.

The Executioner closed his eyes. He would still have time to call Jimenez first thing in the morning, before Grimaldi arrived. So with the Beretta in his right hand and his left forearm resting across the bridge of his nose, he let the street sounds below and the bed springs rising and falling on the other side of the thin hotel room wall be his lullaby. He drifted off to sleep.

5

New Symbionese Liberation Army Colonel Delbert Washington was in his element. He had grown up in this ghetto of Selma, Alabama, and maybe half of the faces he now saw hanging out around the government housing project looked familiar.

"Go ahead, Field Marshal Pentad," Washington said from the passenger's seat of the van. "Just pull up over the curb and drive right on in."

Chad Kauffman, III, shot a nervous glance Washington's way, and the black man suppressed a smile. Chad "Field Marshal Pentad" Kauffman was a rich white boy who loved the title he'd given himself. He preached racial equality, and an idealistic anarchy where everybody treated everybody else fairly because they were treated fairly themselves. But he still hadn't quite come to terms with being the only white guy around.

In Washington's opinion, little Chaddie was scared out of his designer boxer shorts.

The van jumped the curb, drove slowly down a sidewalk between the buildings and emerged onto the sparse muddy grass in the center courtyard of the housing project. As Kauffman navigated the vehicle around benches, discarded mattresses, stripped vehicles and other garbage, Washington looked up at the windows of the apartments surrounding them. Less than half still had glass in them. Some had been covered with plywood or cardboard. Others had simply been left broken with razor-edged shards of glass still sticking out of the frames.

Washington's long rap sheet included several burglary convictions, and he registered the fact that broken windows meant easy entry. But he quickly cast aside such thoughts. The people who inhabited this place, and the hundreds of other projects just like it around the country, didn't have anything worth stealing, unless you counted drugs. And dope was rarely left lying around. It was sold, smoked, snorted, or swallowed as fast as it came into their hands.

Seeing a group of young men gathered around the ripped-out back seat of an automobile near the middle of the courtyard, Washington said, "Pull up next to them, Field Marshal." Again, he had to stop himself from laughing at the title. Kauffman's grandfather, or great-uncle, or some such relation had been one of the fringe members of the original Symbionese Liberation Army back in the 1960s. And for some reason, this spoiled rich kid now driving the van had decided it was his destiny to take up the torch and carry on where those old hippy idiots had left off. Some of the fools had accidentally blown themselves up. Others had been shot down by the cops.

Washington didn't know what had happened to Kauffman's relative. What's more, he didn't care. All he knew was that he'd finally hitched his trailer to a rising star. Little Chaddie might be unrealistic, he thought, and short on common sense, but he had his own kind of smarts. The white boy knew how to plan, organize and talk. That silver tongue of his could have brought out the anarchist in old Abe Lincoln himself, and in addition to the core group Washington was part of, Kauffman had wanna-be revolutionaries planted on university campuses and other places all over the country. The NSLA had established drug contacts in Mexico, and they were expecting a big shipment of coke to come into the country through McAllen, Texas.

The men doing that job had the perfect disguise. They not only all looked like college frat rats, they *were* college students.

Washington chuckled to himself as he thought of it. The college boys he and Kauffman dealt with often irritated him. But sometimes they were amusing. Stupid white sons of bitches had any sense they'd just go to school like their daddies had told them to, then take over the family businesses and live the good life. Instead, they wanted to play Che Guevara and Pancho Villa. Well, he could play the game, too. And he intended to keep playing it as long as he kept getting something out of it for himself.

When things finally started to get hot—and he knew they would—he'd just disappear with all of the money, weapons and anything else of value he could carry. Delbert Washington's mother hadn't raised any fools. He'd let the rest of the group take the heat.

Racial equality, my ass, the NSLA second in command thought to himself. Not in my lifetime.

Kauffman brought the van to a halt and turned nervously toward the man in the passenger's seat as the black men in the courtyard began moving toward them. Washington saw the white boy's eyes flicker to his side, and watched Kauffman's mind register the fact that the door was unlocked. He could almost see the wheels turning in the young man's head as he wondered whether he should reach out and lock it. Would such an act be taken as an insult? Would the black men consider him no better than the crackers all around them in this Southern city?

Perhaps more importantly, would they kill him if he *didn't* lock the door?

Washington smiled at his meal ticket and said, "Don't worry. What we're about to give these dudes is gonna make them forget all about that pale skin of yours."

Kauffman's facial muscles relaxed. But only slightly. "You…uh…" he said. "I think it might be best if you took the lead."

"No problem, Field Marshal," Washington said. "I'm gonna crawl back there and get things started." He unbuckled his seat belt and moved between the seats. "You might want to get back here, too. But stay behind me." He nodded toward the walkie-talkie in Kauffman's lap. "Just man the lines and let me know when it's time to take off."

Kauffman gulped as he nodded.

Washington crawled past the assorted canvas weapons bags just behind the seats and moved to the rear of the vehicle. Next to the back doors sat a ten-gallon aluminum bucket filled with small rocks of crack cocaine. On his knees now, he smiled down at the bucket as he twisted the doorknob and swung both back doors open. He had never smoked crack himself, and never intended to. He'd seen what it did to people who took it up—it took total control of their lives. He'd stick with drugs *he* could control. A little marijuana and beer every day, and the occasional toot of white powder up the nose suited him just fine. The crack he was about to dispense was for controlling the imbeciles.

By the time the doors were open several of the young men were waiting. "Whatchoo doin' here, bitch?" a tall man with a deeply lined face said. A homemade crack pipe stuck up out of the front breast pocket of his shirt.

Washington sat back and said, "Whoa, brother!" He held both hands up, palms outward. "Before you start callin' me a bitch, come see what I got for you." Reaching behind him, Delbert Washington pulled one of the small samples of crack out of the bucket and held out his hand.

The tall man looked down at the crack with a mixture of lust and suspicion. "How much?" he asked.

"Nothin'," Washington said. "Free sample. Fact is, we got free samples for everybody who wants one."

The tall man snatched the rock with one hand as his other grabbed the pipe out of his shirt pocket. "You're Delbert Washington," he said as he dropped the crack into the pipe's bowl.

"That's me," Washington said. "Thought I remembered you, Fishbone. Been a long time."

By now the man called Fishbone had lost interest in the conversation and was holding a small butane lighter over the pipe. His chest seemed to grow to twice its size as he inhaled. His eyes closed and the hard look on his face began to relax as the drug took effect.

Other palms were suddenly reaching out toward him, and Washington began dropping more of the free samples into them. Tiny flames broke out all around the back of the van as more pipes were lit.

Fishbone quickly finished the rock he'd been given and stuck his hand out again.

"Okay, my brother," Washington said, dropping another free sample into the big palm. "But only 'cause we're old friends. After this, everybody has to get a first one before I hand out seconds."

Fishbone nodded, more interested in the rock than fair play. "You dudes movin' into the area?" he asked as he dropped the tiny speck into his pipe.

"You betcha," Washington said. "After today, it ain't free. But we'll beat anybody else's price. That's a promise."

Fishbone took another long hit as more hands thrust forward to accept the free crack cocaine. "The Bow Street Bloods ain't gonna be too happy about that," he said as he finally let the smoke back out of his lungs.

"Bow Street Bloods can go screw themselves," Washington said.

The comment brought several gasps from the crowd now pushing toward the back of the van. Through the quickly closing gaps between the bodies, Washington could see more residents of the project running toward them as word of the free crack spread.

"Bow Street Bloods don't scare us," Washington said as he grabbed another fistful of samples and continued to hand them out. "Business goes to the one with the best product and the best price, huh?"

Fishbone didn't respond. He was too busy sucking more smoke into his lungs and gazing dreamily off into space.

Behind him, Washington heard the walkie-talkie crackle. Then a voice over the air waves said, "L-Three to One. Several cars are headed toward you," Micah Strong said over the radio. "Saw a couple of rifle barrels through the windows."

Washington felt a hand on his shoulder. Then the tense voice of Kauffman said, "Did you hear that, Colonel? The Bloods are on their way."

Washington didn't bother to turn as he went on handing out the crack. By now there were at least three hundred people pushing toward the back of the van. The smell of crack cocaine smoke filled the air, and several fights had already broken out as people jockeyed for position toward the free dope. Fishbone had been pushed out of the way several minutes earlier, a smile on his face that told Washington he couldn't have cared less.

The hand on Washington's shoulder shook harder this time. "Colonel, do you think—"

"Yes, Field Marshal," Washington said. "I think it's time we took off."

Several of the people behind the outstretched hands heard the words and lunged desperately toward the van. Washington was pushed farther back and felt the bucket against his back. "Get behind the wheel," he told Kauffman. A surge of fear shot up his spine. In Washington's experience, nothing was more dangerous than a junkie with a monkey on his back, and he had just whetted the appetite of several hundred of them. The heads and torsos of several men were pushing into the van.

"Start this thing up," Washington said over his shoulder, hoping he hadn't waited too long. "Move back, my brothers. There's enough for everybody."

Kauffman ground the ignition several times and, for a moment, Delbert Washington feared the frightened white man would flood the engine. Then the engine flared to life, and Washington reached behind him, pulling the bucket around to his front.

Dozens of hands shot toward him, grabbing at the contents of the bucket and spilling the small samples of crack over his knees. Washington pushed the bucket into the arms of a light-skinned young man wearing a ragged gray sweatshirt. He reached up and shoved the man's shoulders. The young man staggered backward and tripped, the contents of the bucket spilling out all over the ground.

"Take off!" Washington shouted at Kauffman. He grabbed the side of the van as the New Symbionese Liberation Army leader threw the transmission in gear and floored the accelerator.

The back doors of the van flapped open and shut as the tires tore up the mud and grass. Through them, Delbert Washington could still see the crowd. But they no longer had any interest in the van, and had dropped to their knees, frantically searching through the mud for the cocaine. "Slow down a minute!" Washington yelled. As the van's speed leveled, he grabbed both doors and pulled them shut, then crawled up to the passenger seat next to Kauffman.

The NSLA leader had left the walkie-talkie on the floor behind them, and Washington heard the crisp static again. "L-Four to L-One," the voice of Ansel Reynolds said. "The Bloods are here. Should we engage?"

As Washington reached back for the radio, he saw Kauffman turn toward him, his face full of indecision. The white boy was a master planner, Washington reminded himself. And he was just fine when the only guns around were in his hands and those of the other NSLA core group. But he wasn't worth a damn when he was outnumbered or the odds were even.

Washington lifted the walkie-talkie to his lips as the van started back down the sidewalk leading out toward the street. "Shoot the sons of bitches!" he screamed.

The sound of gunfire could be heard almost immediately.

Washington reached out and grabbed Kauffman's arm. "Better let me drive," he said. "If I was you, I'd get my white face into the back and stay down."

Kauffman frowned as he tapped the van's brake. "But—"

"These brothers ain't likely to know what a wonderful good-hearted integrationist you are," Washington told him. "We did what we came for. No sense in pushing our luck now."

Kauffman nodded and ducked into the back of the van. Washington slid behind the wheel.

A few seconds later the NSLA second in command had guided the van back out to the street. The gunfire had increased, and to his left he could see Micah Strong, Ansel

Reynolds, Sheila Brown and several other members of the core group. They had engaged four cars filled with men in a gun battle—men he could only guess were the Bow Street Bloods. The NSLA members and most of the Bloods had taken refuge behind their vehicles, firing a variety of auto- and semi-auto weapons over hoods and around bumpers. But several of the gang members who had come to find out who was encroaching on their drug territory lay dead next to the cars. One man, the top of his head blown off, was slumped over the steering wheel of a big Lincoln Continental.

Still clutching the walkie-talkie, Washington lifted it to his lips. "L-Two to all L units. Disengage! Repeat! Disengage! Proceed to the prearranged meeting place!"

As the van's tires bumped back down over the curb to the street, Washington turned to the right, away from the ongoing battle. In addition to the gunfight, and the people still running toward the courtyard for free crack, a general pandemonium had engulfed the overcrowded neighborhood. Fistfights could be seen up and down the street as old scores were settled. In front of a small café, several men were beating a man on the ground with scrap lumber and other clubs of opportunity.

Glancing into the rearview mirror, Washington saw flames begin to rise through the broken windows of one of the topstory apartments. The NSLA second in command grinned. They had accomplished what they'd come for. A riot had been the whole reason Field Marshal Pentad had brought them to this ghetto in the first place.

Turning sharply into a run-down shopping center just past

the café, Washington saw people trying to get a look at what was happening down the street without endangering themselves. He didn't know how things looked at the other end of the chaos but unless something was done it looked like the violence might end here. So, cruising along the storefronts, Delbert Washington stared through the windows.

"What are you doing?" Kauffman said timidly from the rear of the van.

"Making sure your riot stays alive, Field Marshal Pentad," Washington replied. The words were no sooner out of his mouth than he saw what he'd been looking for. Pulling to a halt in front of a huge window with the words *Bargains!* and *Sellout!* and *Prices Marked Down!* painted on the glass, he reached into the back seat, unzipped one of the canvas bags and pulled out one of the MP-5 submachine guns they had used at the bank in Oklahoma.

The heads of the people in the parking lot were facing away from Washington as he stepped out of the van. "Hey!" he yelled at the top of his lungs.

Most of the spectators turned toward him, freezing in place when they saw the gun.

"Anybody want a free TV?" Washington yelled. Then, before they could respond, he turned and fired a steady stream of 9 mm hardball rounds through the glass window, opening the appliance store for all.

Several of the younger men in the parking lot had already reached the store by the time Washington got back behind the wheel. As he drove away, he looked into the rearview mirror again. This time, instead of fire, he saw several youths running out of the store carrying television sets.

Kauffman waited until they were a good half mile away from the action before he crawled back up into the passenger's seat.

"An excellent operation, Field Marshal Pentad," Washington said as the rich boy straightened his clothing and tried to do the same with his dignity. "Your plan went like clockwork."

Kauffman took full advantage of the statement. "Yes, Colonel Washington," he said. "Which is why you were correct to suggest I stay out of sight in the back." He stared straight ahead but Washington knew the man was watching for a reaction out of the corner of his eye. "Planning is crucial. And while I realize that some day I will have to pass the baton to someone else, I cannot—with due respect to all—say that any of you are at the point yet where you could take over."

"Certainly not!" Washington said. "Without you, Field Marshal, the New Symbionese Liberation Army would die. Generals cannot lead from the front. They are far too important to the overall war effort."

Kauffman nodded and they drove on. Sirens began to sound behind them.

As Washington pulled the van up an access ramp to the highway, he took a quick glance at his "leader." The rich white boy was still shaken up, but he'd bought Washington's story about generals and the overall effort.

The van pulled onto the highway and, as they disappeared into the busy Selma traffic, Washington fought to hide another smile. Yes, Little Chaddie believed he was indispensable.

What was even more amazing was that Washington agreed.

6

The Executioner awoke to more moderate street noise than that which had lulled him to sleep earlier that morning. Glancing at his watch, he saw that it was nearing eight a.m.

Bolan rose from the bed and walked toward the window looking down upon the street. The neon lights that had burned through the thin window shade the night before were now dark, and the daytime street pedlars had emerged to crowd the sidewalk. The tourists were different, as well. Instead of lusty young men looking for tequila and prostitutes, the Executioner now saw the fathers, mothers and children that made up vacationing American families in search of piñatas, turquoise and silver jewelry, and other Mexican souvenirs.

Taking a moment to gather his thoughts, Bolan continued to stare down at the street. It was a perfect time to call Jimenez. Although he doubted he'd be put through directly to the head of the Mexican crime syndicate—or the front man if what Jorge had told him was true—he thought he might get lucky. He might only get a secretary or some other flunky within the criminal organization, but that didn't matter. All he needed to do at the moment was lay some groundwork. He wanted to perk Jimenez's interest enough that the man decided to check him out. The Executioner would let the criminal record and other red herrings Kurtzman had sprinkled through computer files around the world do his talking for him. The cybernetics expert "Bear" had also flagged all of the files he'd tampered with so word would come back to him if anyone checked on them.

With a little luck, they might even be able to identify whatever cops or military contacts Jimenez had on the payroll.

Five minutes in a shower that sprayed like an old man with an enlarged prostate gland had the Executioner as clean as he was going to get until he returned to Stony Man Farm. Running a razor from his shaving kit quickly over his face, he wrapped a towel around his waist and returned to the bed. He was reaching for the receiver when it rang.

Bolan lifted the instrument to his ear, "Hello."

"And hello back at you," Barbara Price said. "You made your call yet?"

"Just getting ready to."

"Well, you'd better get on it, then," the Stony Man mission controller said. "Jack's circling the airport right now, waiting on permission from the tower to land."

"I can't very well do that while we're still talking," Bolan said.

Price laughed. "Excuse me, big guy. I'll get off and let you get to work. I'll just go back to doing my nails."

Now it was Bolan's turn to be amused. While Barbara Price always looked beautiful and impeccably groomed, she was all business when she was on duty. No one the Executioner had ever met could coordinate the various aspects of complex missions like Price, and she was as valuable to the Farm as any other person who worked out of it.

"Don't forget your hair," Bolan said. "I'll see you when I get in." Reaching for the buttons on the aged rotary phone, he pressed them down for a second, then let up. He didn't know quite how Kurtzman had rigged it, but he got a dial tone. He began dialing the number for the Jimenez hacienda.

A female voice answered on the third ring. *"Buenos dias,"* the woman said. *"Jimenez residencia. Mi nombre es Marina."*

Bolan cleared his throat. Then, speaking Spanish with his best Russian accent, he said, "Good morning, Marina. My name is Anton Mikhailovich. I am calling from Miami to speak with Señor Jimenez."

"Is Señor Jimenez expecting your call?" the woman who had identified herself as Marina asked.

"Nyet," Bolan said. "Pardon me, I meant no. But I believe I have some business that could be mutually profitable to the two of us."

"Please wait while I see if Señor Jimenez is in," Marina said. The Executioner heard a click putting him on hold.

As he waited, Bolan went over the story he had come up with as he'd drifted off to sleep a few hours earlier. Even though Jimenez might not be the true head of the criminal organization, he had to pretend he didn't know that since that was the general consensus of the public. And probably most of the Jimenez organization itself.

Thirty seconds later, Marina was back on the line. "Señor Jimenez is in a meeting," she said.

The Executioner knew that could mean one of two things.

Jimenez really could be in a meeting. But more likely, he simply had no intention of talking to a strange man over the phone. So far, the call was going down exactly as he'd expected. "I would be happy to call back at a more convenient time," he told Marina.

"Perhaps he could return your call," said the woman on the other end.

"That would be excellent," said Bolan. He glanced down at the scrap of paper on the nightstand and read off the number to the prepared line at Stony Man Farm.

The bait had been thrown out, but now, Bolan wanted to set the hook.

Still using the Russian accent, he said, "Please tell Señor Jimenez that I am the owner of a...what should we call it? An import and export business. Yes. That is good. And I specialize in live cargo."

There was a pause on the other end of the line as Marina took in the double meaning. Then she said, "I will pass that information along."

"Also, if you would please, tell Señor Jimenez that he is welcome to check my background. The name is Anton Mikhailovich." He spelled both names. "I am originally from St. Petersburg, but I have been an American citizen for almost two years." He stopped talking and visualized the woman writing the information down. Bolan knew there would be countless Russians with the name Anton Mikhailovich. But Jimenez now had enough variables to narrow things down to the false records Kurtzman had planted.

"Thank you for your call," Marina said politely.

The Executioner glanced at his watch. "I will be out of my office for a few hours," he said in closing. "But I should be back late this afternoon." That would give Grimaldi time to fly him back to Stony Man Farm. And give Jimenez time to reach whoever his police contacts were and run a background check on his Russian identity.

"I will tell him," Marina said, and hung up.

Bolan replaced the receiver in its cradle, tossed the towel into the bathroom and began to dress. He had left his main duffel in the Wrangler, and was forced to put on the same shirt, pants and safari jacket he had worn the night before. Glancing into the bathroom at the all-but-worthless shower, he realized it mattered little. At Stony Man Farm he would clean up and outfit himself for the mission ahead.

Double-checking the Beretta under his arm, the Desert Eagle on his hip and the TOPS SAW clipped into his pants at the small of his back, Bolan left the room and started down the stairs. He had prepaid when he'd checked in, and the long-distance call would never appear on the hotel phone bill. He nodded as he passed the clerk, then stepped out of the lobby onto the sidewalk.

The Wrangler was still where he'd parked it the night before and, unlocking the door, he slid behind the wheel. The vehicle had belonged to Lopez—who had no further need of it—and he would abandon it at the airport.

Fifteen minutes later, the Executioner pulled into a parking space in the lot outside the small airport terminal. Jack Grimaldi, wearing his usual faded leather bomber jacket and brown suede bush pilot's cap, was standing across the tarmac next to one of Stony Man's Learjets. The pilot waved him toward the plane when Bolan started toward the terminal, then walked forward to meet him. The soldier set down his bag when the two met halfway between the plane and the parking lot.

"Customs has already been taken care of," Grimaldi said, smiling. "Amazing what a hundred dollars American can do in the right hands." He reached down, grabbed the Executioner's bag and turned toward the plane. "You entered Mexico illegally," he said over his shoulder. "I didn't see any sense in making you go through the process of trying to leave in a more legal manner." When he reached the Learjet, he flipped open the luggage compartment. "You get any sleep?"

Bolan had followed right behind him. "More than usual," he said as he handed Grimaldi his carry-on.

"Good. Maybe you can catch a few more winks on the way home," the pilot said.

The Executioner nodded as he pulled himself up into the passenger seat. Grimaldi radioed the tower, and a few minutes later they were taxiing down the runway before rising into the air.

"You gonna have time to stay over or are you setting out again today?" Grimaldi asked as they leveled off above the clouds.

The Executioner shook his head. The truth was, he really did need a few more hours of sleep to be in top form. He just wasn't sure he could afford them. "Be leaving again tonight," he mumbled as the purr of the plane's engine lulled his eyes closed.

A second later he heard Grimaldi say something else. But by then he was only half conscious and couldn't answer. And a moment later he was out once more, taking advantage of another rare opportunity to rest before what he suspected would be several more twenty-four-hour days.

7

He still remembered his given name, of course. But as time went by, Chad Kauffman had begun to think of himself as Field Marshal Pentad.

It was time, however, to slip back into his former identity—at least long enough to establish an important contact and further the cause of the New Symbionese Liberation Army.

As Washington pulled the van to a halt on the street outside the fraternity house, Kauffman thought back over the past two years. He had dropped out of Cornell in his junior year after coming up with the idea of restarting the Symbionese Liberation Army while on an LSD trip. It was hardly his first time on acid. But until then, all he had seen were bright colors, cartoon images and other entertaining but meaningless nonsense.

But that trip had been different. It had decided not only his future but his destiny.

As Washington jerked on the parking brake, Kauffman thought back to that night. He had seen and heard an original Symbionese Liberation Army leader speaking to him. The vision had made him realize how his nostalgia for the 1960s—

a period in American history in which he had always believed he belonged—had led him to this point. His mission was to take the name of Pentad, the title of field marshal and to revive the organization.

Chad Kauffman, III, had been seeing a counselor already—paid for, of course, by Chad Kauffman, II. So, under the false impression that his psychologist was bound by oath to keep his plan a secret, he had discussed his sessions with the man. Dr. Randall Bernard had considered his mission criminal, and it was only then that Kauffman had learned that the doctor-patient confidentiality law included only past crimes. Dr. Bernard had threatened to expose his intent to rob banks, distribute drugs, organize campus unrest and other riots, and eventually overthrow the oppressive government of the United States if his patient made even one overt action toward carrying out such a plan.

So Dr. Bernard had become the first man Field Marshal Pentad had killed. It had been easy sneaking through the old bachelor's bedroom window one night and cutting his throat. And while Pentad knew he was a soldier, and should never kill except in the line of duty, he had also found out another interesting aspect of his personality.

He enjoyed killing people.

Washington cut the van's engine and looked over at Kauffman. They were dressed similarly, wearing dark slacks, sport coats, button-down Oxford cloth shirts and expensive Gucci loafers. If it were actually the 1960s, Kauffman knew no black man would have been caught dead in such an outfit. But things had changed over the years. And the fraternity house they were about to visit, while still primarily white, had several black members in good standing. Washington would have no trouble fitting in.

Both men got out of the van, slamming the doors behind them. As Washington tapped the remote control attached to the key ring to lock their weapons and other gear inside, Kauffman patted the pocket of his sport coat to make sure the sample was there. The gesture made him think of the cocaine on its way into the country from Reynosa, Mexico, and he frowned. He should have heard from the men in charge of that deal by now, and he couldn't help wondering if something had gone wrong. He reminded himself to contact Bruce Littner, the NSLA man who had been in charge of picking up the coke in Mexico. Along with bank robberies he and the other members of the core group pulled off, the New Symbionese Liberation Army depended on drug sales to finance both the recruiting of new members and the ongoing operations that would eventually bring down the repressive United States government.

Pushing the troublesome thoughts to the back of his mind until later, the NSLA leader focused on the present. Side by side, like true brothers who knew no skin color, he and Washington mounted the concrete steps to the old three-story building. Kauffman pushed the doorbell and heard the loud chimes behind the double doors.

A few seconds later, a young man dressed as a girl answered the door. Kauffman tried not to smile as he took in the lad's wig, lipstick, short skirt and high heels. A pledge, obviously being punished for some minor infraction of the rules.

It reminded Kauffman of his own fraternity days at Cornell, and the fun, if purposeless, existence he had led there.

"Sirs, I am Pledge Judy, sirs," said the young man, blushing in humiliation even through his makeup. "Sirs, may I help you, sirs?"

"We have an appointment with Steve Hammer," Kauffman said.

The pledge opened the door wider and ushered them in. "Sirs, I will announce you, sirs," he said. Then, eyes down, he began mounting the broad staircase directly behind the front doors.

For a moment, Kauffman thought back to the Porsche he had sold to help finance the start of the New Symbionese Liberation Army. If he was honest with himself, he missed it. Perhaps when the NSLA became more solvent, he would buy another. Right now, he was finding that life on the run cost even more than the lavish lifestyle he had experienced growing up.

The walls of the entryway were covered with photographs, plaques and other awards, and as they waited Kauffman busied his mind reading the honors. Meaningless garbage, for the most part. Fundraising for the United Way, some kind of program providing Christmas toys for indigent children. The same crap his own fraternity had engaged in so they could pat themselves on the back and cleanse their consciences of the guilt that came from being born into money. The same hollow good deeds that Field Marshal Pentad had once believed in when he'd been Chad Kauffman, III, and the same vacuous absurdity that kept his father sending monthly checks to the post-office box he believed forwarded the money to Chad in Ethiopia.

A child of the sixties, Chad II had not taken much convincing that it was time for his son to "find himself." Especially when his son had promised that after a two-year stint in the Peace Corps he would return to college and finish his degree.

The truth was that in two years Field Marshal Pentad hoped to have created enough chaos that there would be no more colleges.

Kauffman believed that only when the country had been reduced to total chaos could a better system be put into place. He didn't know exactly what that system would be, but he knew it would never come to pass until men like Kauffman and Washington had torn down the old government.

The sound of footsteps turned Kauffman's head around again and he saw Pledge Judy coming down the stairs. "Sirs, Mr. Hammer will see you in his office." He turned to lead them to the fraternity president. Kauffman stared at the boy-girl's back as they followed.

Fraternity President Steve Hammer's office was also his bedroom, and was located on the third floor of the old Colonial-style house. He met Washington and Kauffman at the doorway and stuck out his hand to both men. "Great to finally meet you, Chad," he said with the fixed smile of fraternities and sororities the country over. "I've been looking forward to it. Our fathers have been friends for years." He shook Washington's hand with the same smile, then turned to Pledge Judy. "Scram, bitch," he said. "Go scrub the kitchen floor or something."

Hammer ushered the two men into his chambers and closed

the door to the hallway. To the right, Kauffman saw the neatly made bed with hospital corners—undoubtedly done by a pledge. The office area was to the left, and equally impeccable. Hammer waved his two visitors to a pair of matching chairs in front of his desk, then dropped into a seat behind it. Kauffman noted that the wall behind the fraternity president was even more cluttered with awards than the fraternity house entryway. A narrow ledge ran behind the desk, filled with trophies for everything from debate to intramural football. The large portrait of a young blond woman—probably Hammer's girlfriend—stood next to a loving cup announcing that the fraternity president had been voted "Greek of the Year."

Hammer's smile brightened into one of genuine pleasure. "So, gentlemen," he said. "I understand you have some interesting...*product* for me."

Kauffman reached inside his sport coat and pulled out a small plastic bag filled with white powder. He leaned forward and dropped it on the desk.

Hammer frowned. "Coke or horse?" he asked.

"Coke," Kauffman said. "Best you'll ever find. But I can get you heroin, too, if you want it."

Hammer opened a desk drawer and pulled out a small straw. Then, reaching for the bag, he opened it and sifted two short lines onto the desktop. Holding one end of the straw to his nose, he snorted the line and the frown on his face turned into a smile. He drew the rest of the powder into his other nostril, then said, "No argument about the quality. How much of this do you have?"

"Three kilos in the van," Kauffman replied. "Wrapped and taped in plain brown boxes." He paused for a second, then chuckled. "So you can send Pledge Judy out for it if you want to."

"And the price?" Hammer asked.

"It's free," Kauffman said. Knowing that he was still so short on money to pay for the special items about to be smuggled across the Mexican border, the word almost caught in his throat. But he knew you had to spend dimes to make dollars, and the cost of the cocaine was insignificant in relationship to what his special shipment would cost. This was an investment in the future. But the fact remained that he still had to come up with a fast money-making plan if he wanted what Jimenez had offered him.

And he did want that shipment. In fact, he *needed* it. Without it, he knew the New Symbionese Liberation Army would fizzle out the same way the original organization had.

"Did you say *free?*" Hammer asked in disbelief.

Kauffman nodded. "That's what I said. All we ask in return is that you get as many of the brothers, their girlfriends, friends, whatever, into it as possible. Like I told you on the phone, I've got big plans for the future of this country, and I'm going to need help."

"And like I told *you* on the phone," Hammer said. "I think you're nuts." He glanced down at the plastic bag still open on his desk, then added, "But I'll take the coke. And sure, I'll hand it out to as many people as I can. No problem."

"Good," Kauffman said. "Sooner or later, we'll ask for a favor in return."

Bolan walked into Stony Man Farm's armory.

John "Cowboy" Kissinger, the Farm's chief armorer, looked up from the disassembled parts of the laser-sighting device he was working on.

"Howdy, Striker," he said, stepping forward to shake the Executioner's hand.

"What toys have you got for me, Cowboy?" Bolan asked.

Kissinger lifted an odd-looking weapon from the top of the table and held it up for the Executioner to view. "You're familiar with this, I assume?"

Bolan nodded. The short, stubby weapon looked half-carbine, half-revolver. It was an Arwen 37. It held a 5-shot cylinder that could be loaded with just about anything.

"I've tampered with it a little," Kissinger said. "It'll fire these pepper spray canisters instead of the tear gas, if you'd rather." He tapped the top of a canvas bag.

"I'd rather," Bolan said. "You can't always count on it downing a determined attacker. But you can count on it more than the tear gas."

"My thoughts exactly," Kissinger said, shoving the bag

he'd indicated as holding the pepper rounds across the table to the Executioner. "There are a dozen hard rubber baton rounds in there, too. As well as the buckshot, of course." Kissinger frowned for a moment, thinking. Then, changing the subject, he said, "Did I hear Barb right earlier?" he asked. "The Americans buying the cocaine were all dressed like... college boys?"

The Executioner nodded again.

"Then the batons may come in handy. If you find yourself on a campus someplace, I doubt you'd want to blow up the dean's listers along with the bad guys." Then, after another pause, his mind returned to weapons and equipment. "Anything else you figure you might need?"

Bolan shook his head. "I've still got a bunch of stuff on board," he said.

"Then let me send something else along with you just for the fun of it," the armorer said. He turned to a smaller table set against the wall. Turning back to Bolan, he revealed a tiny .22 Short Mini-Revolver. The miniature firearm disappeared in Kissinger's fist before he opened his hand again and extended it to the Executioner.

"First, I filed off the front sight. You don't need it anyway, and this way you can carry it anywhere you want and not worry about it snagging on the draw. Or shoot it through a pocket if need be."

"Go on," Bolan prompted.

Returning to the small table, Kissinger lifted two small red ammo boxes. He passed these to the Executioner as well.

Bolan frowned. "Cowboy, this thing shoots .22 Shorts. These rounds are—"

"Yeah. I know, .22 Long Rifle," Kissinger cut in. "But open the box and take a look at them before you say anything more."

The Executioner opened one of the flaps and withdrew one of the .22-caliber cartridges.

Kissinger had filed down the full lead bullets until they could barely be seen at the end of the brass. The bottom line was that they were the same overall length as .22 Shorts. But the bullets themselves were far lighter, and with the power and force of the more powerful .22 Long Rifle casing, they'd carry at least three times the knockdown power.

"What you've got there is a very small projectile traveling at a very high rate of speed," Kissinger said. "It's still not something you'd want to shoot elephants with. But at close range, you stick that little barrel in somebody's nose or ear or eye, they're going down for the count."

Returning to the side table, Kissinger lifted another small canvas bag and set it in front of the Executioner. "Inside are two more boxes of ammo—that's a total of two hundred rounds. And there's some other stuff."

Bolan unzipped the bag he'd just been handed. He dropped the Mini-Revolver and ammunition in on top of the rest of the little .22's accessories. "I guess that's it, then," he said, picking up all of the equipment Kissinger had provided. "I'm heading for the shower while Jack refuels and does his maintenance check."

He had turned toward the door when it opened on its own and Kurtzman wheeled himself into the room. He was followed by Hermann "Gadgets" Schwarz, the electronics wizard of Stony Man Farm's Able Team.

"Not so fast," Kurtzman said when he saw Bolan had been about to leave. Gadgets and I have a little joint project going you might like to try out." He reached into the pocket of his slacks and came out with a handful of change. He plucked a quarter from amid the pennies, nickels and dimes, and handed it to Bolan.

Schwarz didn't speak. But the Executioner could see the excitement in his eyes.

Kurtzman said, "Take a close look at that thing."

Bolan looked down at the coin. It was one of the series of state commemorative coins, this one honoring Texas. It looked, and felt, no different than any other quarter he'd handled over the years.

Until he turned to look at its edge.

The Executioner squinted. Barely visible through the serrations on the edge of the coin, he could see a line no wider than a hair.

"Now," Kurtzman said. "Tap it on the table."

Bolan did but nothing happened.

"Harder," Kurtzman coached. "We didn't want it to throw off its disguise unintentionally."

Bolan tapped the coin three more times, each a little harder than the last, before a thin wire fell out and began to unravel from within.

Schwarz could no longer hold his excitement at their invention. "Now, grab the end of the wire and tug on it. *Gently*. You don't want to yank it off."

Bolan did as instructed and the wire suddenly stiffened, pointing up in the air.

"Now," Schwarz went on, "look at the face and push the word 'Liberty' just under George Washington's chin. Then hold it to your mouth and call for Barb."

Bolan frowned but continued to follow Schwarz's instructions. He had already figured out what the quarter had to be, but it was taking a little time to believe. "Striker to Stony Man Base," he said into the front of the quarter.

"Now," Kurtzman cut in, "push 'In God We Trust' and then stick it in your ear. I mean that literally rather than pejoratively."

The Executioner pushed the motto with his thumb, then jammed the coin into his left ear. The antenna bent slightly but stayed upright. "Come in, Striker," he heard Barbara Price say.

"You can talk back to her without even taking it out of your ear," Schwarz said. "It picks up the words through the vibrations in your jaw."

"Hi Barb," Bolan said.

"Sounds like its working," Price said. "Stony Man out."

Bolan smiled as he removed the tiny radio. "Show me the rest," he said.

The man showed him exactly how to work the coin.

"Just carry it in your pocket with your other change," Schwarz said. "It hides in plain sight."

Bolan pocketed the tiny transmitter-receiver unit. "What's the range?" he asked the two men.

Schwarz's face fell momentarily. "It's limited," he said. "We're still working on that." He pointed at the Executioner's pocket. "But with that one you've got, you should be able to stay in touch with Grimaldi, at least. And who knows? If the weather conditions are good, and the satellites are in the right place, you might be able to call home just like E.T." He paused for a moment, then added, "But let's put the emphasis on the word *might*."

The Executioner nodded his understanding. "I'll have my cell, too," he said. "But this could come in handy if I need to go undercover, and I've already done that once on this mission."

Kurtzman was nodding, too. "Have fun with it," he said. "Just don't count on it to work as well as a larger unit. At least not until Gadgets and I have had a chance to work on the concept some more."

Bolan thanked all three men, then turned toward the door. He had his hand on the doorknob when he suddenly felt a vibration against his left thigh. Reaching into his pocket, he pulled out a handful of coins, then plucked the Texas quarter from among them. He extended the antenna, stuck the radio in his ear, and said, "Striker here."

Barbara Price's voice came through loud and clear. "You've got a phone call, Striker," the mission controller said. "A Mr. Jimenez to speak to Mr. Mikhailovich. I've got him on hold."

9

Bolan looked down at the blinking light on Barbara Price's phone. Then, lifting the receiver to his ear, he punched the button with an index finger. "Good day, Señor Jimenez," the Executioner said with a heavy Russian accent. "I am delighted that you have returned my call."

"I assure you that the pleasure is all mine, Señor Mikhailovich," said the voice on the other end of the line. "And may I compliment you on your grasp of the Spanish language. My secretary assures me that you are more fluent than most of my fellow Mexicans."

Bolan chuckled into the phone. "One must have at least a working knowledge of many tongues when he is in businesses such as we are," he said. "So…should we get down to that business? I must assume that a man of your power and influence has the ability to double-check my background, and has already done so. Otherwise you would not have called me back."

"This is true," Jimenez said. "I have indeed verified your story. But let us not rush into things. I do not wish to offend, but there are at least three possible explanations for what I learned about your past."

"Oh?" Bolan said. "May I ask what they are?"

"There is always the chance that you were arrested in America, and are facing a long prison sentence. It is not unusual for the gringos to then blackmail a man into turning on his friends and business acquaintances."

"That is true," Bolan said. "I believe they call it 'rolling them over.'" He cleared his throat. "But I assure you, that is not the case with me."

Jimenez continued. "It is also possible that you are a member of one of the American law-enforcement agencies. The DEA, FBI, perhaps even the CIA or Homeland Security. If so, your people are more than capable of planting a false trail for me to find."

The Executioner paused for a second, then chuckled again. "Now it is I who do not wish to offend you, Señor Jimenez. But I can only conclude that you have been watching too many action movies."

The statement made the Mexican laugh, and Bolan laughed with him. But the Executioner didn't kid himself into thinking Jimenez was convinced. The man was still suspicious, and it was going to take more than the planted criminal record to overcome that suspicion. "You said three possibilities," Bolan said when the laughter had quieted. "What is the third?"

"That you are, of course, exactly who and what you claim to be," Fernando Jimenez said.

A short pause ensued. Finally, Bolan broke the silence. "Señor Jimenez," he said. "It is my belief that you and I can make money together. So tell me—what must I do to convince you that I can be trusted?"

"As I have already said," Jimenez answered, "we should not rush into anything. We must get to know each other before either of us can be trusted, no?" Without waiting for an answer, he went on. "I would like to invite you to my hacienda in Mexico City for a few days. Please come down as my guest. We will drink, swim in the pool and get to know each other. Then, perhaps, we can discuss business."

"It would be my honor," the Executioner said. "When would my arrival be convenient?"

"Come as soon as you are able."

"I will do that. I can easily adjust my schedule, and will have my pilot begin making preparations immediately."

"Excellent!" Jimenez said. "I will await the honor of your presence, and have men waiting for you at the airport."

"Until then," the Executioner said.

The bait had been taken.

JACK GRIMALDI SET the wheels of the Learjet down on the runway and slowed the plane to a stop. Bolan unbuckled his seat belt, staring ahead through the windshield toward two vehicles parked on the tarmac. One was a brand-new Mercedes-Benz. The other was an older Ford sedan that, although unmarked, bristled with too many antennas to be anything but a police or military vehicle. Three hard-looking men got out of the Mercedes.

At the same time an obese man, in a tight-fitting white tropical-weight suit, struggled out from behind the wheel of the Ford.

Across the parking lot, Bolan saw a Jeep heading their way. Behind the wheel, the Executioner could see a man garbed in a khaki military uniform. The Jeep reached the group as Bolan opened the door to the plane and swung down.

The khaki-clad officer started to climb out of the Jeep carrying a clipboard. But before he could hit the ground the fat man in the white suit stepped forward and held up a badge. Shrugging, the customs official drove away again.

The Executioner walked forward to greet the quartet waiting for him.

"Welcome to Mexico," the fat man said in Spanish. "I understand from these men that you have great command of our language."

"I do my best," the Executioner said in his Russian-accented Spanish.

"I am Captain Felix Garcia," he said. "I came only to simplify your entry into our fine country by eliminating customs," Garcia went on. He waved toward the Jeep, which was just arriving back at the small private plane terminal. "So, my work here is done." He turned his back to Bolan, held out his hand, and one of the other men handed him a white envelope. Without further ado, he squeezed himself back into the Ford and drove away.

The man who had handed Garcia the envelope stepped forward and extended his hand to Bolan. "My name is Petre Obregan," he said as they shook hands.

"Anton Mikhailovich."

Obregan nodded. "Señor Jimenez asked me to extend his apologies in advance," he said as he dropped Bolan's hand. "But we must search you for weapons before we take you to him. He was sure you would understand."

"I understand," Bolan said, raising his arms. "And I can save you some trouble. Look under the left arm, on the right hip and at the small of the back."

Obregan stepped back as one of the other men—this one wearing a bright yellow shirt—stepped forward. He jerked the Beretta from the Executioner's shoulder rig, the Desert Eagle from the holster on his belt and the knife from the sheath behind him. Handing the weapons to the third man, he continued his frisk. He tapped Bolan's crotch tentatively, and the Executioner said, "Don't get too excited there."

The comment turned the man's face purple. He muttered under his breath and quickly moved his hands on.

Finally, turning to Obregan, he nodded.

"Shall we proceed to the hacienda, then?" Obregan said, smiling.

"That's the reason I came," Bolan replied. He turned briefly toward the Learjet where Grimaldi had opened the luggage compartment and was setting his bags—those that contained clothing rather than weapons—on the ground. "Stay here and check her out, Jack," he told Grimaldi in his Russian accent, but using English this time. "I don't know how long I'll be."

Grimaldi started toward the pilot's side of the plane again. "Yes, sir, Mr. Mikhailovich," he answered, smiling. Grimaldi would stay on call, close to the plane's communications center.

Obregan opened one of the back doors to the Mercedes and ushered the Executioner inside. As he rounded the rear bumper, he called out to the man who had frisked the Executioner. "Pedro! Get Señor Mikhailovich's luggage."

Pedro nodded, apparently still slightly offended at the Executioner's slight to his masculinity. He refused to look their way as he walked to the plane for the bags.

Bolan was pleased at the man's discomfort. It had moved his searching hands quickly away from the Executioner's crotch, which had been Bolan's reason for the insult.

Obregan climbed into the Mercedes on the other side of the Executioner, and the other two men got into the front seat. A few minutes later they had left the airport and were cruising along a thoroughfare into the city proper. With the Mexican presidential campaign still underway, billboards and other signs favoring either the incumbent or his challenger seemed to appear every few feet. "Have you been to Mexico City before, Señor Mikhailovich?" Obregan asked.

Bolan had, many times. But he doubted that Anton Mikhilovich would have, so he said, "Only the airport. When switching flights."

Obregan nodded, pulling a crumpled package of cigarettes from his shirt pocket and offering one to the Executioner. Bolan shook his head as the Mercedes rolled on, bumper to bumper with other modern automobiles, some ancient relics held together with baling wire, and even the occasional horse-drawn wagon.

The highway twisted north and, if anything, the political signs for the presidency seemed to increase. "As you can see, we have an election coming up," Obregan said. "I doubt that it interests you. The president, Jose Marquez, and his challenger, Julio Martinez, appear to be closely matched. The last I heard, Martinez was slightly ahead in the polls."

"The only interest I have in politics is how they might affect business between Señor Jimenez and me," Bolan said.

Obregan's face took on a strange smile, which made the Executioner wonder what the man was thinking.

The two men in the front seat had remained silent during the drive. That did not change as the driver pulled the Mercedes onto an exit ramp into a suburb. Soon they were passing guarded gates that led to elaborate haciendas hidden from the road by carefully trimmed trees, hedges and shrubbery. Each villa appeared to sit on several acres.

At last the Mercedes turned into one of the gates. A high stucco wall, and two guards carrying M-16s slung over their shoulders, suddenly appeared just beyond the first curve in the driveway. The men recognized the Mercedes immediately, and an iron gate in the wall began to swing open. The guards saluted as the vehicle passed by them. None of the men in the Mercedes bothered to return the gesture.

It took a full two minutes to drive from the street up the winding concrete path that led to the house. They passed row after row of carefully tended sycamore trees, an orange orchard in full bloom, and several ponds filled with goldfish. Finally, they crossed a wooden bridge spanning a running stream before finally turning into the circular driveway in front of the house. As the driver stopped the Mercedes just outside the elaborate front entrance, Bolan looked out his window to see a three-story palace.

"Welcome to the Hacienda de Jimenez," Obregan said as he got out of the Mercedes. "If you will follow me, Señor Jimenez awaits your presence in the courtyard." Then, turning to the man in the yellow shirt, he shouted, "Pedro! Get the gentleman's luggage!"

Pedro continued to mumble under his breath.

The Executioner got out of the Mercedes as the third man opened his door for him and followed Obregan into the house. Bolan was led through the opulent hacienda and on to the courtyard. The Jimenez gunman opened the door, stepped back to let the Executioner through, then closed the door again behind him.

Bolan stepped out onto the courtyard and stopped. Seated on a bench on the other side of the swimming pool was a short stocky man with dark skin. The man wore carefully pressed white linen slacks and a matching shirt, unbuttoned to the waist to expose a smooth chest and a large silver crucifix.

Jimenez had a book in his lap. A small handbell and a drink of some kind sat on a metal end table just to the side of his bench. He looked up over the top of the reading glasses perched on the end of his nose as Bolan and Obregan approached, then set the book down on the bench next to him, folded the spectacles into his shirt pocket and rose to his feet.

"Señor Mikhailovich," Jimenez said. "It is my honor and pleasure to have your company." He extended his hand and held it out in the air as Bolan stopped in front of him. He was about to speak again when the door to the conservatory opened behind them and a maid stuck her head through the opening.

"Yes," Jimenez said, nodding as he spoke to himself. "Forgive my manners. Can Josefa get you something to drink? You are Russian. A vodka, perhaps?"

Bolan looked at Jimenez's glass on the bench. "Whatever you're having is fine," he said.

"Josefa!" Jimenez shouted. "Another tequila on the rocks for our guest." He glanced to Obregan, who had stopped just behind the Executioner. "Please, do not think I am rude to my employees. They are not allowed to drink while working. Actually, you are treated quite well, are you not, Petre?"

Obregan smiled. "As long as we perform our duties well, we are treated like guests rather than employees," he said dutifully.

"Thank you, Petre." Jimenez beamed. "But, speaking of employees, where are Carlos and Pedro?"

"They have taken Señor Mikhailovich's bags to his room," Obregan reported. "They will be down shortly."

The words were no sooner out of the man's mouth than the door opened again. The other two men who had driven Bolan from the airport appeared along with Josefa carrying a tray filled with glasses.

"Please," Jimenez said. "Sit down."

Bolan took the chair to Jimenez's left. Obregan—who was clearly Jimenez's right hand—and the other two sat. No one spoke as Josefa served first Bolan and Jimenez, then handed tall glasses of what looked like a mixture of iced tea and lemonade to the three henchmen.

As soon as the maid had retreated into the house, Jimenez said, "I hope I did not offend you by having my men take your weapons?"

"Not at all," Bolan said. "I'd have done the same thing."

At that prompt, Pedro rose from his seat and walked forward, pulling the Beretta, Desert Eagle and TOPS SAW knife from under his baggy yellow shirt. He handed them to Jimenez without speaking, then returned to his seat.

"Hola!" Jimenez almost shouted as he hefted the big .44 Magnum pistol in his hand. "We can go hunting if you'd like—I have plenty of land in Mexico. But I am afraid you will find no elephants outside of the zoos in this country."

Bolan politely exaggerated a laugh. "I like to be careful," he said. "Just like you. And I've always found that big guns bring down small game better than trying to make little guns kill big game." He paused for a moment, then said, "Particularly the kind of large game that walks upright on its hind legs." Then, after another short pause, he said, "May I have them back now? My holsters get lonely without them."

A look of false sadness came over Jimenez's face. "I am sorry," he said, shaking his head. "Perhaps soon, though. First, we must establish more of the trust we spoke about on the phone." He set the pistols and knife down on the bench beside him, *away* from the Executioner.

"So how do we go about establishing that trust?" Bolan asked.

"I have been going over and over that very subject during your flight down here," Jimenez said, tapping his temple with a forefinger. "And I believe I have come up with a plan."

The Executioner smiled. "I don't know what that plan is. But I might have one that doesn't take as long."

Jimenez looked quizzically at the Executioner as he rose to his feet. He looked even more puzzled when Bolan stuck his hand down the front of his pants.

John "Cowboy" Kissinger had provided Bolan with a jockstrap, the type worn by baseball catchers with a built in pocket for a hard plastic cup. But instead of the cup, Stony Man Farm's chief armorer had sewn in a small leather holster for the tiny .22 single action Mini-Revolver.

The befuddlement on Jimenez's face turned to shock when Bolan brought the little gun up and over his belt, thumbed back the hammer, then turned and aimed the stubby barrel at Petre Obregan, seated at his side. "I could have already killed you if that's what I wanted to do, Señor Jimenez," the Executioner said. "There are five shots in here. I could have killed you all."

Before anyone could react or reply, Bolan un-cocked the Mini-Revolver, leaned forward and handed it butt-first to Jimenez. "See for yourself."

The dark skin of Jimenez's face had gone gray as he took the gun in both hands and looked down at it. Then, gaining control of himself, he handed it back to Bolan. "You are correct," he said. "Had you wanted me dead, you could have done it. So you may as well have this, and your other weapons, returned." Twisting to the side, he picked up the Beretta as Bolan placed the .22 back into his jock holster. The Executioner slid the 93-R back into the shoulder rig and tucked the knife back into the sheath at the small of his back, as Jimenez picked up the Desert Eagle. Bolan waited, but the man hesitated for a moment, studying the huge .44 Magnum pistol once more.

Finally, Jimenez looked up at Obregan. "Who searched this man, Petre?" he asked.

"Pedro," he said.

Without another word, Jimenez lifted the Desert Eagle, pointed it at the man in the yellow shirt and pulled the trigger.

Jimenez behaved as if suddenly killing one of his own men was a daily occurrence. Casually, he flipped the Desert Eagle's safety back on and handed the weapon back to the Executioner. "As Petre said, my employees are treated like guests when they do their jobs well," he said as he pointed down to the body only a few feet in front of him. "But this is what happens when they do not."

Bolan shrugged indifferently. "I guess it's a good thing I'm planning to be your partner instead of your employee," he said.

The remark brought a laugh from Jimenez. Looking to Obregan, he said, "Please, Petre. You and Carlos rid us of this disgusting sight, won't you?" He waved down at Pedro's body. "And tell Josefa she has some cleaning to do when we are finished out here."

Obregan and Carlos got to their feet quickly. With Carlos taking Pedro by the ankles and Obregan grasping his wrists, they began hauling the body away. Obregan looked back for a moment, his eyes darting back and forth from Jimenez to the Executioner, his face a mask of concern.

Jimenez waved him on. "Go on," he said. "Señor Mikhailovich has no plans to kill me. If he did, I would already be dead due to Pedro's incompetence. I would like to speak with him privately anyway."

Again, Obregan looked from his boss to Bolan, and it was obvious he was not as comfortable with the situation as Jimenez. But he shrugged and went back to helping carry the body through the glass door.

Bolan waited until they were gone, then said, "So, shall we discuss business?"

Jimenez chuckled under his breath. "Not yet, señor," he said. "You have proved only that you do not wish me dead." He took a sip from his glass of tequila. "But neither would a police officer of either Mexico or the United States." He set the glass down again and said, "Now you must prove that you do not wish to arrest me and put me on trial."

"And how do I prove that?" the Executioner asked.

"Let us have another drink," Jimenez said. "Then, I shall tell you."

Josefa appeared again as if by magic. She took a quick glance at the bloodstained patio but her face betrayed no emotion whatsoever. She delivered fresh drinks, then disappeared into the house again.

"So tell me," Bolan said as he tasted the new drink.

"I will," Jimenez said. "But, first, you tell *me* what sort of joint business you believe we can do together."

"All right," Bolan said, setting his tequila on the table next to him. "I'll prove that I am as trusting of you as you are untrusting of me by being blunt. I bring illegal immigrants into the U.S. from Eastern Europe. Russia, Ukraine, Romania, all of the countries of the old Soviet Bloc. I bring them in by sea. And I've yet to be caught."

Jimenez nodded. "So," he said, taking another sip from his glass, "if you are so successful on your own, what would you want with me?"

"I can do the same thing with illegal immigrants from Mexico," Bolan replied. "And Mexico is a lot closer to the U.S. than Poland."

Jimenez nodded slowly. "Which would be cheaper and

raise the profit margin," he said. "Even with me as an equal
partner." He lifted his glass toward his lips, started to take a
drink, then changed his mind. "But you must know that I
smuggle far more than illegal aliens," he said. "And that these
immigrants are at the very bottom of the smuggling trade in
terms of profit."

"Yes," the Executioner said. "I know that. In fact, my guess
is that the illegals are more of a diversion than a moneymaker.
So I figure that once you and I get things in place, we move
from indigent farm workers to drugs. Cocaine. Heroin. Top
grade marijuana. With the THC content in the twenty-percent
range now, marijuana prices are hand-in-hand with coke."

"I do not need a partner for such operations," Jimenez said
simply. "I already have them in place."

The Executioner paused a moment, wondering if he should
play the ace up his sleeve at this moment or save it until later.
He didn't know for sure but his gut told him that if headway
wasn't made immediately, there might not be any later. So,
with a deep breath, he said, "The reason you need me, and
the setup I've already got in place, is *because* you have a partner, Señor Jimenez. And that partner takes far more than the
fifty-percent cut I'll be asking for." He paused to watch the
Mexican's reaction.

Again, Jimenez had been about to take a sip of tequila but
stopped. As Bolan watched, the man's olive skin began to turn
gray once more.

"Maybe the general public doesn't know there's a silent
partner behind this operation," the Executioner went on. "And
while your top men like Obregan probably know, I doubt

most of them know exactly who it is." Again, he waited to watch the other man's reaction.

Jimenez's frozen hand slowly thawed. He set his glass back down. "Are you telling me that you know?" he asked, for all practical purposes admitting that there was indeed another man above him.

Bolan waited, thinking, calculating. If he told this front man that he *did* know the identity of the real power behind the Jimenez organization, it might put him in a better bargaining position. But if he claimed that knowledge, Jimenez was likely to demand a name. And when the Executioner couldn't give one, the man sitting across from him might react badly.

"No, I don't know who it is," Bolan said, then quickly added, "And I don't want to know. That part of your life is none of my business. What I'm proposing would be just between you and me, Señor Jimenez."

The color was coming back to Jimenez's face now. He lifted his glass, threw the remainder of the tequila down his throat, then set the glass down a little harder than was necessary. "I think it is time you began calling me Fernando, Anton," he said, smiling.

Bolan nodded. "Then we have a deal?" he asked.

Jimenez held up a hand. "Probably," he said. "But let us not rush into things. You have perked my interest. And I do not believe you plan to assassinate me." He stopped talking for a moment, lifted his glass, then remembered it was empty and set it back down again. "But that does not mean I can trust you in other ways."

"With all due respect, Fernando," the Executioner said, "I must ask you to explain."

"For the sake of argument," the Mexican crime boss said, "let us assume that you *do* represent a law-enforcement agency of some type, either Mexican or American. If so, you would not be sent here to murder me but to build a criminal case which could be tried in a court of law." Jimenez lifted the hand bell and shook it.

Josefa appeared through the door to the house so quickly that she had to have been standing just inside, waiting.

"Bring Señor Mikhailovich and me another drink please, Josefa," Jimenez said. "Make them doubles...no, just bring us two new frosted glasses and a fresh bottle. I think we may be here awhile."

Bolan turned his attention back to Jimenez. "All right," he said. "Again—for the sake of argument only—let's assume that I'm an undercover agent of some kind. How do I prove to you that I'm not?"

10

He had learned of the busted cocaine deal from a story on the Internet. It seemed that some sort of disagreement had occurred between two unidentified groups, one Mexican, the other American, just south of Reynosa. Every last one of his men—along with the Mexicans—was dead. That explained why Bruce Littner had not contacted him.

The remains of the Americans who had gone south of the border to pick up the coke, were awaiting identification before being shipped back to the United States.

Kauffman was surprised by his own reaction to the news. Littner and his men were expendable, so their deaths did not bother him. He had dozens more men just like them. But the money the coke deal would have brought in was essential to the cause, and his first reaction to the news had been a near-panic. A quick phone call south of the border had assured him that his contact there was as mystified as to what had happened in Reynosa as he was. They had done business together too many times to suspect each other, and together had come to the conclusion that the *federales* had stumbled across the deal, killed both sides, stolen the money and found another buyer for the cocaine.

But the intact trust between Field Marshal Pentad and Fernando Jimenez did nothing to help the NSLA treasury. Now, now more than ever, Pentad knew he had to come up with some other way to finance the special shipment Jimenez was about to send his way. The Mexican smuggler had told him that the specialty items he had ordered had arrived, and were now stored safely in Mexico City. They were awaiting the final details—like payoffs to the *federales*—before being shipped north to the border.

In the meantime, Field Marshal Pentad was running short of both time and money.

Kauffman leaned back in his chair for a moment and closed his eyes. None of that was the part of his thinking he'd found surprising. What was curious was that he'd suddenly realized that the old axiom, "Necessity is the Mother of Invention" held true.

He could hardly believe that he hadn't thought of kidnapping earlier.

Kauffman opened his eyes again and felt himself smiling. The snatch he had in mind should be easy, and would bring in more money than if he pulled a bank job and sold cocaine every day for a year. It would also coincide nicely with the official announcement he was about to make to the United States of America in order to refocus the country's attention where it belonged. Not on ill-conceived threats of terrorism from the Islamic countries in the Mideast, but on the injustices being carried out every day, right here at home.

Kauffman lifted the scissors on his desk and snipped the final letter of his communiqué to America from a magazine.

Dabbing a small amount of glue on the back, he pasted it to the page. He took a deep breath of satisfaction, then sat back in his chair to view his work. The message, which was about to be sent to the *New York Times,* was short and simple:

To the Current Repressive Government of the United States:

Be it known that the Symbionese Liberation Army, thought by you to have been destroyed years ago, has reemerged with new strength and spirit. We are responsible for the acts of patriotism listed at the end of this communiqué, as well as the kidnapping yesterday of Sue Ellen Waters. We will not cease our actions until the racist, sexist and arrogant leaders of the United States have been overthrown and re-placed by men and women who represent the people of America rather than big business, political factions, and the other selfish interests who are now in power.

Kauffman felt himself nodding in agreement with his own words. He had been tempted to place his true signature at the bottom of the page but better judgment had cautioned him that it was not yet time for that revelation. Instead, he had used more letters, cut from magazines, to end his proclamation simply:

Let the Revolution Continue!
Field Marshal Pentad
The New Symbionese Liberation Army

Kauffman rubbed the fingers of his latex gloves together to dry the glue they'd picked up during the pasting process. Then, carefully folding the page so as not to dislodge any of the letters, he placed it in the envelope. The address had already been glued to the outside with the same magazine letters, and he grinned as he looked at the upper-left-hand corner of the envelope which read, "Forever Moving." That return address had come as an afterthought, but he liked it.

Kauffman sealed the envelope by running a damp sponge across the flap. Human saliva, he knew, contained DNA and while he knew the government had no other sample of his DNA for comparison, sooner or later they would guess who he had to be and obtain one from his parents' home or his old room at the fraternity house. Eventually, he knew the entire world would find out that Field Marshal Pentad had begun life as Chad Kauffman, III. And he *wanted* the world to know. Just not yet.

Kauffman sensed the presence of someone behind him, and now he started to hand the envelope over his shoulder. But another thought hit him suddenly, he jerked it back, then turned.

Washington stood just behind his chair, his ungloved hand outstretched, ready to take the communiqué and mail it.

Kauffman took a deep breath and thrust his meager chest outward as his narrow shoulders squared importantly. "Colonel Washington," he said in the official sounding military tone he had heard in hundreds of war movies, "does it make sense to you for me to go to all of this trouble to conceal my fingerprints and then plaster *yours* all over the communiqué?"

Washington lowered his head and bit his lip in shame. "No, Field Marshal," he said, sounding suitably chastised.

Kauffman smiled inwardly but kept the expression off his face. "Look at me, Colonel," he said in the same voice of importance.

Washington's eyes rose, his face looking like that of a man who might be about to hear that he would soon face a firing squad. His top teeth continued to bite into his lower lip, like they frequently did when Kauffman had to correct some mistake on his part.

"I *know* that you have been a political prisoner for the last several years," Kauffman said. "And that, as such, you have not been able to keep up with the advancement of law-enforcement forensics."

"Yes, Field Marshal," Washington replied. His words were stronger but still contrite. "That is true."

"When you were incarcerated," Kauffman went on, "fingerprints were only useful when a suspect had already been identified and samples could be rolled for comparison." He took another deep breath. "But during that time, the imperialistic pigs have come up with what they call AFIS—the Advanced Fingerprint Identification System." He raised a fist to his lips, coughed more for affect than anything else, then continued. "Now, they can run even a partial print through this AFIS system and have their computers kick out the five-to-ten most likely candidates."

Washington lowered his head again. "I have heard of this AFIS," he whispered. "But I was not certain what it did."

Washington's remorse for the foolish action he had been about to take fueled Kauffman's confidence, and he squared his shoulders again. "Well, now you know," he said. "Anyone whose prints have ever been taken—whether it was after an arrest, upon entering the military, or for any other reason—and entered into this system are now at the fingertips of the police." Realizing what he had just said, he forced a smile. "You will pardon the pun, please."

Washington returned the smile. "And my fingertips have most definitely seen the ink pad, Field Marshal," he said.

"Precisely my point," Kauffman said. He nodded toward the box of surgical gloves on the table next to him.

Washington slid his hands into a pair of rubber gloves. Kauffman could see the man's dark skin through the thin stretchy fabric and the fact that it even registered in his mind embarrassed him.

Was such an observation racist? Should he not even notice such differences between Washington and himself? He didn't know. But he knew such thoughts confused him, so he forced them from his mind. Handing the envelope to the man in front of him, he did his best to get the obvious fact that Washington was black out of his head. "Cover what you are wearing now with leather or wool or cotton or some other type of gloves before you post it," he said. "We do not need someone seeing you drop it in a mailbox with those on. And *do not* mail it until our mission tonight has been carried out. If some unforeseen obstacle prevents our success tonight, I want to be able to try again tomorrow."

Washington transferred the letter to his left hand and then snapped a smart salute. "Yes, Field Marshal," he said.

Kauffman nodded as he rose from his chair. "At ease," he said. "So…shall we proceed with the evening's operation?"

"Everyone is ready," Washington said.

Kauffman slid his arms into a plain gray raincoat that easily covered the HK MP-5 submachine gun hanging from the shoulder sling across his back. "Then let us begin," he said.

"To the Revolution!" Washington said loudly, saluting again.

Field Mashal Pentad returned the salute. "To the Revolution!"

SOMETIMES HIS ABILITIES made Delbert Washington think he should have taken up a career on stage or screen instead of turning to crime. Then again, the average movie-watcher probably wasn't as gullible as this white boy he saw before him now, cutting up magazines like some five-year-old in kindergarten art class, then pasting the pieces on a sheet of paper as if he were the Unibomber or Zodiac Killer or some kind of James Bond who'd just stolen a secret code from the Red Chinese.

Washington had waited patiently while Kauffman went into what Washington had begun to think of as his Patton voice. The stupid little white boy sounded just like George C. Scott playing that part in the movie *Patton*. Washington had to have seen the film a dozen times when he'd been in prison. It was one the warden had loved to show, hoping it might inspire patriotism which, in turn, would inspire one or more of the convicts to turn their lives around. As far as Washington knew, the only thing it had ever inspired was several shankings. The dark theater combined with the loud combat audio gave inmates a perfect setting in which to settle old scores and escape undetected.

When the speeches began, Washington knew it was time

for him to get into his respectful second in command character. Although he knew more about DNA evidence and fingerprints than Kauffman ever would, Washington had decided it was best to allow the white boy to correct the imagined mistake and let him pump up his delicate ego.

They had left the cheap motel room and were headed toward their newest stolen vehicle, a dark green, nondescript Toyota parked just outside the door. Sheila Brown was already behind the wheel, and through the windshield of the van parked next to the Toyota, Washington could see the faces of Micah Strong and Ansel Reynolds. Strong was behind the wheel, and the NSLA's number two knew that as soon as they neared the bar where they'd find Sue Ellen Waters, Reynolds would get into the back of the vehicle. A new toy had been brought across the Mexican border by some of Kauffman's campus revolutionary wanna-bes, and Washington had spent a good part of the night installing it in the van.

That "toy" was an M-60 machine gun that Kauffman's contacts south off the border—Jimenez was the name of the guy if he remembered right—had stolen off a Mexican armored car or tank or something. But regardless of where it had come from, the big gun was now mounted in the back of the van, the barrel facing the back doors. Washington had used a welder's torch to cut out a small hole in one of the doors, enabling the gun to be fixed with only an inch of barrel sticking out of the vehicle. It could fire directly behind the van without even exposing the weapon. If a wider range of fire was needed, the doors could be opened.

Either way, the M-60 had been a great idea in Washington's

estimation. That might be, he laughed to himself, because he had thought of it himself. Maybe it would keep this ragtag group of college fools out of jail until this "big weapons deal" Kauffman kept hinting about finally bore fruit. Washington didn't know exactly what this deal consisted of. But if his own plans went well, he'd have disappeared from the NSLA a rich man before any of it ever went down.

Kauffman got into the passenger's seat of the Toyota and Washington slid into the back. Like the field marshal himself, he was wearing one of the cheap gray raincoats they'd picked up at a discount clothing store months earlier and worn to conceal their weapons during the bank jobs. Beneath both coats were their MP-5s. Washington also had a Colt Python jammed into his pants. He didn't know what pistol Kauffman had chosen from the group's arsenal but he knew he'd have some kind of backup weapon.

Sheila Brown gave Kauffman a quick kiss on the cheek as she backed the Toyota out of the parking lot, then led the way from the motel to the access ramp leading onto the highway. A few minutes later, they were cruising past the first exits to Austin, Texas. Washington studied the back of the coffee-skinned neck beneath Brown's wild Afro hairdo. The woman had worn dread locks when Kauffman had first recruited her into the core group of the NSLA. But he'd talked her into the 1960s style within the first week. It had taken *days* to get the kinks and tangles worked out of those locks, and Washington still hadn't figured out what the black woman saw in this white boy that she'd go through all that for him. She was smart enough to know that this stupid

NSLA thing couldn't last forever, and that when it was over little Chaddie would most likely be cut off from Daddy's money, one way or another.

Did the sister have her own agenda? Probably. If so, maybe he'd wait until he got what he wanted, then cut her in on things and they could both just disappear.

Almost as quickly as the thought had entered his head, Delbert Washington pushed it out. There were plenty of sisters around for a dude like him with money. No sense in cutting it up with this one. Let her stay with Kauffman, and continue to make the white boy believe he was a true nonracist by sleeping with a black chick.

Washington waited patiently while Brown took the exit, then turned onto the path leading to the University of Texas. Soon, they were caught up in the heavy traffic cruising past the restaurants, bars, book shops and other businesses that could be found around any college campus. Washington caught himself grinning as he watched the pedestrians on the sidewalk. Many were couples making their way along the strip from one watering hole to the next. Others were groups of young women, dressed to attract the groups of young men who were also on the sidewalks, looking for them. It was little different than the areas around any of the college campuses Kauffman had dragged him through during the past several weeks as he recruited NSLA members with free drugs.

When they had reached their destination, Brown pulled to a halt behind a row of parked cars. Both men opened their doors. Even before they got out, the sound of horns blasting in the traffic stalled behind them began. They ignored the noise and anger. It was unavoidable. Besides, a good traffic jam would keep the cops at bay longer.

Kauffman opened the front door to the Black Cat Saloon and held it back while Washington walked inside. The NSLA second in command had to keep from laughing again. The field marshal was never first through any door. He preferred to let his black deputy take such risks and let it play out as nonracism.

Finding himself in a dimly lit entryway, Washington moved inside just far enough to allow Kauffman to follow him and close the door. Beyond another door, he heard loud music blasting forth from what sounded like a live band. Behind a small table, wearing a white pullover polo shirt, designer jeans, black lizard cowboy boots and a matching belt with a huge rodeo buckle, stood a young man who called out, "Five bucks cover charge, gentlemen. Each."

Washington saw no reason to kill the man but evidently Kauffman did. The explosions behind him came as something of a shock as he watched the doorman twist and jerk to the time of the 9 mm rounds pouring into his body. Either the rock and roll in the next room covered the shots, or the patrons of the Black Cat thought it was all part of the show, because the musicians didn't miss a beat and played on.

Keeping his MP-5 covered with his raincoat, Washington opened the door and stepped into the large bar. The band was set up at the other end of the room, atop a stage just off the dance floor. Between the dancers and where he stood were dozens of tables, most of them packed with college boys and girls and covered with pitchers of beer.

Kauffman stepped up next to him. "You remember what she looks like from the picture?" he asked.

Washington nodded. "But we'll never find her in here," he said. In truth, Sue Ellen Waters general description fit maybe thirty percent of the young women inside the Black Cat. But Washington couldn't resist adding, "All white people look the same to me."

Next to him, he heard Kauffman chuckle nervously.

"Don't worry," Washington said. "I know how to find her."

"How?" the NSLA leader asked.

"I could tell you," Washington said, throwing the tail of his raincoat back to uncover the MP-5, "but it'd be easier to just show you." Raising the submachine gun on its sling, he aimed the barrel at the ceiling and flipped the selector switch to full-auto. A second later a long burst of fire peppered the roof.

Inside the main room now, the sound of gunshots was unmistakable. The band came to an abrupt halt on a sour note. The chatter around the tables cut off just as fast, and the dancers seemed to freeze in place on the dance floor.

"But what do we do now?" Kauffman was able to whisper.

"Just walk forward and do your thing," Washington whispered back. "Tell them who you are, and what you want." You're good at *talk,* he thought. It's the *walk* that gives you problems.

Kauffman stepped forward. "I am Field Marshal Pentad of the New Symbionese Liberation Army," he shouted in a voice with a slight tremble. Then, without having to be prompted further by Washington, he fired his own burst of 9 mm rounds just over the heads of the band.

The musicians dropped to the floor almost as if they'd been hit.

"Silence!" Kauffman yelled above the screams and shrieks that followed the gunshots. His voice held more confidence now. "I want Sue Ellen Waters, and I want her *now.*"

The patrons in the Black Cat heeded the first order and silence fell over the barroom once more. But when none of the girls stepped forward, Kauffman looked down at the nearest table.

Washington followed his eyes and saw a group of huge, beefy men who he pegged as university football players.

"You!" Pentad shouted, his voice becoming more fearless with every word. "Stand up!"

A man with biceps and triceps bulging out of his tight shirt pointed at his own chest.

"That's right," Kauffman shouted. "You!"

The man stood up.

"Point out Sue Ellen Waters," Kauffman screamed. "Now!"

"I don't know any Sue Ellen—" the big man started to say.

Kauffman cut off the sentence with another burst of fire that struck the football player in the chest, knocking him back over the table behind him. Even in the dim lighting, Washington could see the occupants of the table try to jerk away as blood flew over them. The screams around the bar returned, then died again.

"Now," Kauffman said, puffing his thin chest out the way he only did once the odds were completely in his favor. "Who wants to tell me who Sue Ellen Waters is?"

At least a hundred index fingers suddenly pointed to a girl seated at the bar.

Washington kept his MP-5 aimed in front of him as he moved swiftly through the tables. The woman being pointed at was doing her best to shrink into her bar stool. She had long, straight dark-brown hair, large eyes that had widened in horror, and wore skin-tight blue jeans, an equally tight T-shirt and snakeskin boots.

Washington grabbed a handful of the long hair and jerked her off the bar stool.

Sue Ellen Waters screamed in both pain and terror. "Help!" she cried. "Won't somebody help me?"

No one did.

A moment later, Kauffman fired another burst from his MP-5, which took out the remainder of the football players at the table in front of them. Yeah, Washington thought. Just the kind of guys a wimp like you would hate. Then Field Marshal Pentad turned his MP-5 toward the stage and cut loose with a steady stream of 9 mm rounds into the musicians hugging the floor. Delbert Washington couldn't help wondering if a guitar player had bedded an old girlfriend of Kauffman's or something.

Groans and moans filled the air when Kauffman finally quit firing. Without another word, he turned and followed Washington out the door.

The car horns on the street were playing a loud and angry symphony as Washington dragged Sue Ellen Waters out of the building. As the second in command neared the Toyota, he heard Kauffman scream, "Shut up!" Then another burst of fire exploded and the glass of several car windows shattered. As the roars died down, Washington heard the scream of a police siren and, a block or so from where they had stalled traffic, the red and blue lights as the patrol car tried to weave in and out of the congested automobiles.

Dropping his submachine gun to the end of the sling, Washington opened the back door of the Toyota and threw the college girl inside the vehicle. By now she was sobbing uncontrollably. He slid in next to her and saw that her eye shadow had spread all the way down her cheeks, making it look as if she was crying brown tears.

As Kauffman jumped into the front seat, Brown said, "The cops are on their way. Should I tell Strong and Reynolds to open up on them?"

"Tell them to do whatever they have to!" Kauffman shrieked, his voice losing the confidence it had gained for a few moments inside the Black Cat.

Sheila Brown lifted a walkie-talkie to her lips, "Take out the pigs coming up behind you," she said. "We're out of here!" She threw the transmission into drive and screeched the tires.

The loud, booming explosions from the M-60 suddenly sounded over the horns, angry shouts of the drivers, and the rest of the noise that had come as a result of the traffic jam. Before Brown turned, Washington saw the black-and-white's windshield shatter and watched the grille disintegrate. Both doors opened, and two men in blue—both looking as if they were already injured—stepped out.

Washington turned to face the front as the Toyota raced away. A moment later, he saw the van make the corner behind them.

Kauffman turned on the walkie-talkie.

Washington heard a screech as one of the men in the van

keyed his transmitter button. Then Ansel Reynolds's voice came over the air waves. "L-Four, here."

"Status report," Kauffman said, his voice trembling again.

There were no such tremors from Reynolds as he answered back, and Washington was reminded that while Reynolds had never done penitentiary time—or even been a criminal before hooking up with Kauffman—the man had the cold hard stare of a much convicted felon. Reynolds, Washington knew, was that rare individual who simply didn't care if he lived or died. He didn't have a death wish. But he had no life wish, either. "One disabled cop car and two very dead pigs," the man said.

"Affirmative," Kauffman replied. "Maintain radio silence from here on out unless there's an emergency."

Washington heard the click as the NSLA leader let up on the transmit button.

"Not a bad night's work," Washington said, glancing at the terrified young woman who sat frozen like a statue next to him.

"No, not at all," Kauffman said. He turned sideways in his seat and stared at Sue Ellen Waters. Then, turning his eyes further to meet Washington's, he said, "But it's nothing compared to what we've got planned in the near future."

Delbert Washington frowned. Kauffman had been hinting at some big time shipment from Mexico for weeks. And he had dropped enough clues that Washington knew what was coming was some kind of weapon, rather than drugs. He suspected that when these weapons arrived, it would be his cue to grab all the available cash lying around and head as far in the opposite direction of the NSLA as possible.

This white boy he saw in front of him had started out on

the verge of insanity. Washington was now ninety-nine percent convinced that the field marshal had finally tipped over
that invisible line.

A moment later, an explosion even louder than those from
the M-60 filled the air behind them.

Washington turned again and saw flames rising toward the
sky from the spot where the police car had been only seconds
before.

11

Daylight was creeping around the edges of the window shade when the Executioner opened his eyes the next morning. He had spent the night in one of the hacienda's several guest bedrooms, sleeping lightly.

The Desert Eagle had rested in his right hand under the covers.

Jimenez had admitted that Bolan hadn't gained his complete trust. And there was at least one thing the Executioner had learned: When the time came for murder, Jimenez preferred to do it when his quarry had their guard down. Jimenez had simply called Pedro into the hacienda courtyard as if he wanted to have a drink and chat with the man. One moment the man was laughing and talking. Then, the next moment, Jimenez had used Bolan's Desert Eagle and the man was dead.

The Jimenez method of operation in eliminating problems was no different than that of most organized crime assassins. They maneuvered their victims into a situation in which they had little hope of defending themselves, then put them to death. And there were few times in a man's life when he was as helpless as when he was asleep. It made perfect sense that if Jimenez really suspected the Executioner of being a cop, or snitch, or intelligence officer, he would send his murderers during the night.

He hadn't.

But Bolan had been prepared for the event should it have happened. He rose to a sitting position and swung his legs off the bed. Even though he had not slept soundly, he felt refreshed. He took in the lavish surroundings of his sleeping quarters. It was like the rest of the hacienda—beautiful and decadent at the same time.

The Executioner's disgust far overpowered his appreciation of the fine antique furniture. How much cocaine, heroin and other drugs had it taken to afford just this one bedroom, let alone the entire Jimenez hacienda? How many lives had been ruined by those drugs? How many men had died of overdoses, or lost their families to the powdered demons? How many people had been murdered, and how many immigrants had slowly baked to death in the back of eighteen-wheelers illegally entering Texas?

Bolan didn't have any answers. He knew there was no way he could bring the dead back to life. He could, however, avenge all those ravaged by the Jimenez organization.

And he would.

Rising, the Executioner lifted the big .44 Magnum pistol and glanced around the room once more. With all of its opulence, it lacked any modern conveniences. There was no computer and, even more conspicuously, no telephone. That didn't surprise him. This was a guest room for guests who weren't trusted, and who were not to have any secret contact with the outside world.

Taking the Desert Eagle with him into the bathroom, Bolan turned on the shower. As the water warmed up, he turned to the sink and saw a new disposable razor and toothbrush. Both were in their original packaging, but he lifted them to his eyes for closer inspection anyway.

Satisfied that neither the razor nor toothbrush had been tampered with, Bolan inspected a can of shaving cream and tube of toothpaste he found in the medicine cabinet above the sink. They looked equally safe so he put them to use.

Steam began to rise from the shower, clouding the mirror, as he lathered his face and began to scrape off two days' worth of beard. He thought back to the late-night conversation he'd had with Grimaldi after finally being shown to his room. Using the Texas quarter radio as soon as he'd been led to his bedroom, he'd passed on to the Stony Man pilot all of the intel on the Jimenez organization he'd picked up so far. That had been done for one simple reason.

Every step forward he took on this mission was another step that might bring on his own death. If that happened, he wanted Stony Man Farm to have a running start when they sent Phoenix Force, Able Team, or another group of warriors to finish what he had started.

As he brushed his teeth, he remembered what Grimaldi had told him about what was happening back in the U.S. Sue Ellen Waters, the daughter of big-time Texas oil baron J. Travis Waters, had been kidnapped from a bar near the University of Texas campus. The men who had taken her had killed several of the bar's other patrons, and loudly proclaimed they were a reincarnation of the old Symbionese Liberation Army of the 1960s. So far, there had been no ransom demand.

The NSLA was now claiming to be the group who had robbed banks all over the Southwest United States and even blown up several police and sheriff's vehicles in Kingfisher, Oklahoma.

Bolan finished brushing his teeth and showered quickly. A few moments later, he had dressed in a clean short-sleeved shirt, light slacks and his hiking boots. Sliding into the Beretta's rig and holstering the Desert Eagle on his hip, he threw on his light jacket to cover the weapons.

He was about to open the door to the hallway when he remembered the tiny North American Arms .22 he had carried in the jock-rig the day before. Now that Jimenez and Obregan knew of its existence, he wondered if it had not lost its value. But on a hunch, he returned to his bags, found the little wheel gun, and pulled it from the jockstrap. Digging further, he located the ankle holster Kissinger had also supplied and wrapped the Velcro straps around his ankle just above the top of his left hiking boot. Pulling his sock up over the rig, the minute weapon all but disappeared, and when he pulled the cuff back down, it did completely.

Jimenez and Obregan were sitting at the breakfast table when Bolan entered the kitchen. Both men had china coffee cups and saucers in front of them. They turned his way as he stepped through the door.

"Ah!" Jimenez said, smiling. "Our guest has arrived!"

Bolan took a seat between the two men, and Josefa set a saucer and coffee cup on the table in front of him. Raising the cup to his lips, he found the strong brew just this side of boiling, took a tiny sip, then set the cup in the saucer to cool.

"I trust you slept well?" Jimenez asked.

Bolan nodded. "Always do," he said, remembering to lace his Spanish with the Russian accent. "Innocent conscience."

The comment brought hardy laughter from Jimenez. Obregan allowed a slight smile.

Josefa returned before the conversation could go further, delivering a large plate of eggs to each man. "We have much to discuss," Jimenez said as he shook a bottle of hot sauce before sprinkling it over his scrambled eggs, onions and ground beef. Then, turning to the maid, he said, "That will be all for now, Josefa."

The woman understood the cue. She quickly left the room.

Bolan took a bite of his breakfast, swallowed, then tried the coffee again. "Must be top secret stuff if Josefa had to go," he said.

"Yes," Jimenez said. "I am sure my house staff realizes I am involved in a few…shall we say *unusual* businesses. And they are well paid to keep quiet about anything they chance to overhear. Of course, they know what will happen to them if they do not." He shrugged. "But why tempt fate? It is still best that they are not privy to all of our details, no?"

Now it was Bolan who shrugged. "Makes sense to me," he said.

"Precisely." Jimenez nodded. Finally satisfied that his breakfast would be hot enough, he set the bottle of pepper sauce down and lifted his fork to his mouth. "And it would be a shame to have to kill a woman who cooks like this, eh?"

Bolan nodded. He was quickly tiring of the small talk and wanted to get down to business. But he knew it was wiser to let Jimenez get around to it in his own good time.

While the two men had been talking, Obregan had been eating, and now he was almost finished. "Did you find the breakfast to your liking, Petre?" Jimenez asked.

Obregan grunted as he took the last bite.

Jimenez chuckled. "That is what I like about Petre," he said, looking at the Executioner. "He is a man of few words. But much action."

Bolan had started to take another bite, but now he set his fork back down on the side of his plate. "Why do I get the feeling that this is leading to *me* undertaking some of your action, Fernando?" he asked.

Jimenez's smile widened. "Because you are a very perceptive man, Anton."

Bolan shook his head slowly back and forth, conveying a mild impatience. "How many of your hoops do I have to jump through before you believe that I am what I say I am?" he asked.

"Just one," Jimenez said.

The Executioner quit shaking his head and turned it into a quick nod. "Good. What is it you want me to do?" Bolan asked.

"I have one test for you. Pass it, and I will no longer question your intentions," Jimenez said, a grim expression on his face.

"And if I don't pass it?" Bolan asked.

Jimenez shrugged. "Then you will die," he said. He set down his fork and raised his coffee cup to his mouth.

Bolan lifted his coffee cup again, and this time he found the coffee cool enough to drink. After he had carefully replaced the cup in its saucer, he said, "Am I correct in assuming you have somebody you want killed?"

"Yes," Jimenez said.

"Who?"

"A man named George Hidalgo," Jimenez said, looking Bolan in the eye as he spoke.

Bolan stared back at the man, waiting for an explanation. When Jimenez remained silent, he finally said, "Who is he?"

"While he has a Hispanic surname, George Hidalgo is not Mexican. He is a citizen of the United States."

"So?" Bolan said. "You forget—I'm only a naturalized American. I'm Russian by birth. American merely for convenience." He paused and took a sip of his coffee. "What did you think I might do? Refuse to kill this Hidalgo character and stand up and belt out a few stanzas of the 'Star Spangled Banner'?"

Jimenez's face cracked into laughter for a moment. "I like you," he said. "Not just your guns but your sense of humor, too."

"Why should this guy being American mean anything to me?" Bolan asked.

"There is more," Jimenez said. "Not only is George Hidalgo not Mexican, he is not involved in any illegal activities whatsoever."

The Executioner forced himself to shrug. He knew where this was going. Jimenez had realized that even if Bolan was a cop or federal agent he might still be willing to kill criminals. Jimenez wanted the Executioner to kill an innocent man in order to prove himself. "If this man isn't part of your organization, and stealing from you, or someone trying to take business away from you," he said, "why do you want him dead?"

Jimenez continued to look the Executioner in the eye, and it was obvious he was doing his best to read Bolan's every reaction to the bits of information he was letting out one at a time. As the grin returned to his face, he said, "An organization like mine has enemies other than our competitors and the traitors within." He sighed, glanced at the ceiling for a moment, then let his eyes fall back to the Executioner's. "George Hidalgo is one of those enemies. But there is a reason why even a rogue American or Mexican agent, willing to bend the rules and shoot criminals, would hesitate to kill him."

Bolan continued to meet Jimenez's gaze as a silence of several second fell over the room. Finally, he said, "So, are you going to tell me what that reason is? Or do we have to keep on playing 'twenty questions'?"

"I will be happy to tell you," the criminal front man said. "The reason an undercover law enforcement officer would not want to kill George Hidalgo is that he is an agent of the United States Drug Enforcement Administration."

Jimenez, having finally dropped the bomb, probed the Executioner's face even harder for a reaction.

When Bolan remained deadpan, he added, "The fact is, George Hidalgo is the special agent in charge of the DEA's Mexico City office."

12

The cabin was only a few miles north of San Antonio and was of the basic A-frame design. It had been built on a ridge near the top of a large hill with only a small and distant view of Canyon Lake carefully cut out through the thick forest that surrounded it.

Kauffman had rented the A-frame because of its isolation. And in addition to the fact that it was invisible from the road, any vehicle driving up the hill to the house had to pass through two padlocked gates upon which Washington had installed motion detectors. Unwanted visitors would be announced a good fifteen minutes before they came calling.

Kauffman leaned back in his desk chair and stretched his arms over his head. In front of him was an instrument that the original SLA had never dreamed of, let alone had at their beck and call, when they'd planned their own campus riots and other disruptions.

A computer.

His arms relaxed, Kauffman returned his hands to the keyboard and typed out another of the instant message communiqués he was sending simultaneously to three NSLA lieutenants on three separate campuses. "These actions should begin as simple peace demonstrations," he wrote. "Demonstrations against America's actions in Afghanistan and Iraq. The police must appear to have instigated the violence themselves." He hit the Send button and sat back, waiting for a reply.

It wasn't long in coming, and it came in the form of a question. "How do we do that?" wrote Bertram Mansfield, the head of the NSLA faction at the University of California at Berkeley.

Kauffman answered him just as quickly. "There are two possibilities," he typed. "The best is to steal a police uniform and assign it to one of your members. Order him to draw his gun and fire into the crowd of demonstrators."

"But won't he be recognized and arrested?" the same lieutenant wrote back.

"Not if he appears suddenly amid the other officers and wears a riot helmet with face shield," Kauffman answered.

"Should he fire blanks?" Mansfield asked.

"No."

"Then he should shoot over the demonstrators' heads?"

Kauffman didn't hesitate. "No," he wrote. "Pick out one or two of your least useful freedom fighters and order the man disguised in the uniform to shoot them."

There was a long hesitation on the other end. So long, in fact, that Kauffman finally wrote again to break the cyber-silence. "Sacrifices must be made," he tapped onto the keys. "No individual is as important as the overall cause. And those who die will be heralded, for all eternity, as martyrs."

"Affirmative" finally appeared on the screen from all three lieutenants.

Kauffman smiled. The loyalty of his leaders was touching. They were willing to sacrifice, and make martyrs of some of their own to further the movement of the NSLA. What they didn't realize was that *everyone* at the peace demonstrations–turned riots would become martyrs. Demonstrators, police, the curious onlookers—*everyone*. And it would, indeed, appear that the police had been the instigators of one of the greatest mass slaughters in history.

But the various campus leaders could not be told this, so Kauffman continued in the same vein as before. "If it is not possible to obtain a police riot uniform," he typed, "then several freedom fighters should be assigned to instigate violence on the part of the pigs. On cue—and remember, the riots should all begin at precisely 3:00 p.m. EST—they should begin by throwing rocks at the police line. These items must be smuggled in and not used until the 3:00 startup time." He folded his hands together, then turned them palms outward, and cracked his knuckles at the screen.

Again, the word "affirmative" appeared three times in the tiny boxes in front of him.

"Now," Kauffman typed, "and this is the most important part of all…" He quit writing for a moment for the sake of drama, then typed, "You will each be receiving several official police-only-issue canisters of crowd control pepper spray. These you will secretly give out to your most trusted disciples only. You will instruct them to activate the canisters as soon as the pigs have begun to use their clubs. Is that clear?" Kauffman sat back and held his breath. The last order had to appear to be almost secondary in nature in order to hide the truth from his campus leaders.

"Clear," came the response from all three colleges.

Then Bertram Mansfield wrote, "So this should appear to be an act of the police as well?"

"Yes," Kauffman wrote back. "That is imperative."

"Can we reach you between now and then in this same manner?" asked Fred Partridge, the NSLA leader at the Massachusetts Institute of Technology.

"Negative," Kauffman responded. "I will be changing screen names for each communiqué. But I will contact you every three hours until Saturday. Beginning Saturday at 0000 hours I will touch base hourly."

When the three lieutenants had confirmed their understanding, Kauffman typed in, "Please reiterate the chief goals on each campus. Johnson, please go first."

Amanda Johnson, the female leader of the NSLA at Colorado State University, sent her instant message. "As soon as the violence erupts, the freedom fighters on this campus will take over, and burn the library building."

Kauffman grinned. Burning the library at CSU had been his idea. It would be reminiscent of what had happened there during a student uprising in 1970.

Mansfield answered next. "Our chief goal will be the administration building," he wrote.

Last came Partridge's reply, short and simple. "Set fire to the field house and adjacent football stadium."

Kauffman heard a low moan from the sleeping loft at the top of the A-frame as he answered with "Correct" to all three of his lieutenants. "We will touch base again in three hours," he tapped onto the keyboard, then signed off and shut down the computer.

Kauffman swiveled in his chair and saw Washington sitting on the couch against the wall opposite the desk. Washington had heard the moaning too, and was staring up the winding steel staircase that led to the sleeping loft. The eyes of his second in command were still filled with the lust they had harbored ever since the NSLA had abducted Sue Ellen Waters from the bar in Austin. Washington had been in favor of stripping the woman naked before they bound and gagged her on the bed upstairs, and Kauffman had been forced to pull rank in order to stop him.

Anarchy, and a new way of life in America and eventually the world, was the goal of the New Symbionese Liberation Army. Not rape, or the selfish satisfaction of any personal lusts. Washington had grudgingly conceded. But Kauffman knew the man still hoped to have sex with Sue Ellen Waters before she was ransomed back to her father. Or killed.

For a brief moment, Kauffman thought of the excitement he felt every time he pulled the trigger of his MP-5 and snuffed out the life of another capitalist pig. But the thought was troublesome, so he forced it from his mind.

Kauffman twisted his head and looked at the telephone next to the computer. "You are *certain* this line is untraceable?" he asked.

"Oh, it's traceable," Washington said. "Just not back to here."

"You're sure?" he asked again.

"I'd bet—I am betting my life on it," Washington said, prying his eyes away from the steps. "All of our lives, I guess." He opened his mouth, yawned, then said, "Like I told you. The dude I celled with for about six months—same guy who taught me how to do the alarm sensors on the road gates— was also an expert at rigging phone lines. Used to work for the phone company."

Nodding, Kauffman had started to lift the receiver when he heard an automobile engine nearing the cabin outside. Even though he knew the alarm would have sounded had uninvited guests broken through the gates, he glanced at the security box resting on the other side of the computer. The light was still green, which meant the approaching vehicle had to be the van, and that either Micah Strong or Ansel Reynolds had tapped the code into both locks before driving through the gates.

Kauffman wanted no interruptions or telltale background noise when he made the phone call he had planned next, so he waited until both Strong and Reynolds had entered the A-frame. The two men carried grocery bags in both arms and set them on the kitchen cabinets at the rear of the ground-level room before exiting to the van for another load. After the third trip, Reynolds closed the door behind him and then joined Strong in emptying the sacks and stuffing their contents into cabinets, drawers and the refrigerator.

When they had finished unloading the supplies, Kauffman said, "I'm about to call the Waters house. Take a seat, both of you. Don't speak, and don't make any noise."

Strong and Reynolds nodded. Reynolds dropped down next to Washington on the couch, and Strong took an over-stuffed easy chair facing the front porch and the distant lake.

Lifting the receiver to his ear, Kauffman listened to the dial tone as his eyes fell to the top sheet of the scratch pad next to the rest of the instrument. Slowly, purposefully, he tapped in the area code and phone number they had obtained from the captive woman.

As he waited for the line to connect, Kauffman heard the moaning begin again. "Shut her up!" he yelled toward the loft where Sheila Brown sat watching the young woman. "I'm making the call!"

The moaning ended as the line was picked up on the second ring. Kauffman smiled to himself, mentally picturing the FBI agents crowding the elaborate living room of J. Travis Waters. He could almost see one of the men in suits grasping an extension phone, then nodding to Waters so they could both pick up the receivers at the same time. A third agent would have an earpiece in his ear and be ready to hit the buttons on a tape recorder and a tracking device.

The FBI was in for a surprise. According to Washington, the call would trace back to a phone booth in Dodoma, Tanzania.

"Hello?" a voice tinged with suppressed anxiety said. "This is J. Travis Waters, speaking. Whom may I ask is calling?"

"You mean you don't have some repressed peasant screening your calls today, Mr. Waters?" Kauffman asked with all of the sarcasm he could muster. "Some black maid who's trying to feed five children on the minimum wage salary you pay her? Or maybe an illegal alien who you can pay even less than minimum wage who can't report you to the authorities for fear of being sent back to Mexico or the Philippines?"

There was a long pause on the other end. Then a gruffer, more confident voice said, "Why don't we cut the bullshit and get down to business? Who are you, and what do you want from me in return for my daughter?"

"Let's take your questions one at a time," Kauffman said. "First, you may address me as Field Marshal Pentad, head of the New Symbionese Liberation Army."

"I know who you are," Waters said. "Every newspaper in the country picked up *The New York Times* story. So how much is it? I'll pay whatever you ask. All I want is my daughter back safe and sound."

"Again," Kauffman said. "You're getting ahead of yourself. We want money, yes—money to further what will one day be seen as the greatest revolution in the history of the world. But there are other demands, as well."

Again, Waters paused, and Kauffman pictured one of the agents giving direction with his hands, or holding up a quickly scribbled note so the oilman could read it. When he finally broke the silence, he said, "Just tell me what those demands are, Field Marshal Pentad."

"First," Kauffman said, "you are to publicly state that you've achieved your obtrusive wealth at the expense of others. That you, and other capitalist pigs like you, have trampled the smaller people of the world so that you could live in your obnoxiously lavish lifestyle."

"Fine," Waters said. "I'll do it, no problem. How do you want it done?"

"I want to hear it on television, radio and read about it in the papers."

"I'll tell them," Waters said. "But I have no way of forcing them to either print my words or announce them. I can't—"

Kauffman had expected such an answer, and he slammed the phone back into the cradle. The action was not out of anger; it was for effect. He waited thirty seconds, then dialed the number again. When he heard the same voice say, "Hello?" he said, "I hope I have made my point. I can cut off negotiations at any time I choose, Mr. Waters. I hold all the cards. Don't tell me you *can't* do anything. A man like you can get the news media to say anything he wants."

Again a few seconds went by and Kauffman suspected there was more silent FBI coaching going on. Then Waters said, "I'll see that it gets done. What else?"

"In order to demonstrate good faith, I want you to make a donation to the American Communist Party. Let's make it for—" he paused for a second, doing his best to make it appear he was searching his mind for a figure "—let's make it for two million dollars. Yes. That's a nice round number."

"Consider that done, too," Waters said quickly. "You'll read about it in the press."

"Yes, I certainly hope I will," Kauffman said. "Or else you'll read about a young woman's body being found somewhere. A young woman who did not die quickly or painlessly." He stopped, again for effect, then said, "I promise we'll leave enough of her to do a DNA match up, though." Waiting a few more seconds for the implication to set it, he finally said, "And there is one other demand. Your daughter will be returned to you upon receipt by the NSLA of ten billion dollars."

"What!" J. Travis Waters gasped into the phone, and Kauffman could tell that was one response the FBI hadn't directed. "You must be crazy! Even a man like me can't raise that kind of cash!"

"Then I suggest you raise all you can and go begging for the rest from some of your rich friends," Kauffman said into the phone. "It'll be good for you, having to beg. It builds character. And it'll let you see how the rest of the world has to live when people such as yourself hoard all of the money."

"I can try," J. Travis Waters said into the phone, and now his voice was trembling with fear. That made Kauffman grin again. He wondered how long it had been since the man had faced a situation he wasn't wealthy enough to handle. "I can try—" the oilman said again. "But my friends won't—"

"Then you'd better find new friends," Kauffman interrupted. "If you can't, you'll still get your daughter back of course. But in *pieces.*"

"Please," Waters whimpered. "Please don't—"

Kauffman cut him off again. "I'll get back to you with the details on delivering the money," he said. "In the meantime, get busy depositing the two million in the ACP account." He started to hang up, then a mental picture of some of the FBI agents scurrying around the Waters living room while others tried to trace the call forced one last statement from him. "And speaking of friends, tell your new federal ones to say hello to all of the citizens in Dodoma."

"Do—what?" Waters said, sounding close to tears. "What are you talking abou—"

Kauffman dropped the phone back into the cradle and

looked up at the other members of the NSLA's inner circle. "Gentlemen," he said. Then, looking up toward the open sleeping loft where he knew both Sheila Brown and Sue Ellen Waters could hear his voice, he added, "And ladies. As Sherlock Holmes used to say, 'The game is afoot.'"

Washington leaned forward on the couch, folded his arms over his knees and said, "You don't really think the old bastard's going to come up with ten *billion* dollars, do you?"

Kauffman shook his head. "Of course not," he said. "But that's nothing but smoke up his ass anyway. It's the two million we need. At least for right now."

Ansel Reynolds stood up and looked down at Kauffman. Then, after a quick glance toward the sleeping loft, he lowered his voice and said, "You given any thought on how we're going to get the girl back to the old man?"

Kauffman glanced as well, again reminding himself that while he couldn't see the woman, they could both hear his voice. So, whispering even lower than Reynolds had, he said, "We're not. The old man will never come up with the ten billion. Besides, did you ever stop to think about the logistics of that amount of money? It would take an eighteen-wheeler to cart it off." He waited a moment, then raised his voice to an audible level again. "But he *will* donate the two million to the ACP to keep the ball rolling. And like I said, that's what we want."

Reynolds frowned. "What good will that do us?" he asked.

Kauffman shook his head in wonder at the man's stupidity. Where would oafs like Reynolds and Strong be if it weren't for men like him and Delbert Washington? "The American

Communist Party has no actual part in this," he finally said. "The money will be wired into an account I've opened in New Braunfels. I'll give the account number to Waters only seconds before the transaction takes place. We'll then with-draw enough to pay for what's coming to us from Mexico, and be gone before the bank even knows what's happened."

"What *is* this stuff you keep referring to from Mexico?" Micah Strong asked.

Kauffman was tempted to tell him, but he wasn't sure how the rest of the core group would take the news that he was sac-rificing so many fellow NSLA members. Better to let them think the same thing the public would believe for a while—that the police had been behind the mass murders on the three college campuses. Later, when the angry reaction of young people all across the country had replenished the ranks and even multiplied them, he might tell them the truth. But for now, he simply gave Strong a big smile and said, "I could tell you. But it would be so much more fun just to show you once we have it."

The answer seemed to satisfy the men in the A-frame, and Kauffman turned back to his computer. Lifting the phone again, he tapped in another number he had jotted down on the note pad and listened to a female voice say, "First Bank of New Braunfels, may I help you?"

"Chad Kauffman, III, calling for Mr. Delano," he said. "He'll remember me. I was in earlier this morning and opened an account."

"Oh, yes, Mr. Kauffman," the girl said. "I remember you myself. Buying a ranch in the area, aren't you?"

Kauffman forced a laugh. "Yes, I intend to become what's sometimes referred to as a 'gentleman rancher.' In any case, I was calling to make sure the cash I'd requested for my wire transfer has arrived."

"Mr. Delano is out at the moment," the girl said. "But I saw the Wells Fargo guards haul it in about an hour ago. It should be ready as soon as the wire comes through."

"Thank you," Kauffman said. "And…what was your name?"

"Gena, Mr. Kauffman."

"Yes, Gena. And please remember that I would like this kept confidential. I'm a very private man and don't like everyone, particularly in a small community like this, knowing my business."

"My lips are sealed."

"Good," Kauffman said. He hung up and sat back in his chair. Feeling far more like Field Marshal Kauffman than he ever had before, he folded his hands behind his head. Two million even was what Fernando Jimenez was charging him for the three phony police-issue crowd control pepper-spray canisters. They had originally been assembled in the Ukraine for use against dissidents, then found their way to the black market after the fall of the Soviet Union. And while that figure was indeed high for pepper spray, it was not pepper spray that the NSLA was actually buying.

Although labeled as nonlethal crowd-control devices, each stationary, self-revolving can actually held VX nerve gas, a single drop of which, on exposed skin, would cause death within ten minutes. Which meant that literally thousands of people in Berkeley, California, Boston, Massachusetts, and

Fort Collins, Colorado, would die during what everyone thought to be "peace" demonstrations.

Including, but unknown to them, many members of the New Symbionese Liberation Army themselves.

13

Bolan took another sip of his coffee and replaced the cup in the saucer. "And when do you want this George Hidalgo killed?" he asked.

"Immediately," Jimenez said. "Petre will take you to—"

The Executioner's shaking head stopped the man in midsentence. "Impossible," he said.

Jimenez stared back at him as he'd been doing all morning. "And why is it impossible?" he asked.

"Because killing a DEA agent—especially a SAC—is going to bring the heat down like you've never seen it before."

"Are you refusing to do it?" Jimenez asked.

"No," Bolan said. "I'm not refusing to do it." He paused, thinking. He couldn't refuse. He had to convince Jimenez he was a Russian-born criminal rather than an undercover operative. If Jimenez didn't buy his cover, he would order Obregan, or another of his gunmen, to kill him.

Or at least try.

It would mean he was no closer to the real head of the Jimenez organization than he'd been when this mission had started. And that the big weapons deal about to go down on the border would succeed.

"I'm not refusing to do it," the Executioner repeated. "What I'm saying is that it's going to take some planning. I'm willing to do it. But only if I can do it right." He paused, took a sip of coffee, then added, "If you don't mind, I think it'd be a good idea to kill George Hidalgo in a way that doesn't wind up with any of us in jail. Or stretched out on a steel table with tags attached to our toes."

Jimenez leaned back and lit a cigarette with a gold lighter. "You realize that I cannot let you out of my—or Obregan's—sight until you have completed this task?"

"Of course I realize that," Bolan said. "You're still trying to decide if I am who I say I am or some deep undercover cop of some kind. I understand that. I'd do the same myself. And if you leave me to my own devices, and I am a cop, all it would take would be a fast phone call to make sure this Hidalgo stayed underground or was on the next flight back to the U.S."

"Precisely," Jimenez said, taking a drag on his cigarette.

Bolan finished his coffee. "As I said, it'll take some planning. I want to see the local DEA offices and the surrounding area before I decide how I want this to go down."

He turned his attention to Obregan. "I suppose you know what this guy looks like, and what his schedule is?"

Obregan nodded. "Like the back of my hand," he said. "As special agent in charge, he is in a management position. Which means he does not work undercover any more and has no need to keep his face concealed."

"What about his working hours?" the Executioner asked.

Jimenez answered the question for Obregan. "Petre has observed him for several months now. He is truly a creature of habit. He arrives at work at exactly eight o'clock each morning. He goes to lunch—at his home, with his wife and a young daughter—between noon and one. He leaves the office again at six, and does not go back at night unless a large drug bust is planned."

Obregan laughed quietly. "Which is one of the reasons I have watched him," he said. "When he returns to the office in the evening, we curtail any large transactions that happen to be in progress." Leaning back against his chair, he folded his hands in his lap. "It means our federal agents—even those on our payroll—are being pressured by the United States to make arrests."

"You said that's *one* of the reasons you've been watching him," the Executioner said, "which implies there are others."

Jimenez stepped back into the conversation. "Just one other one," he said.

"Which is?" Bolan asked.

"To kill him," Jimenez said simply, knocking the ash off the end of his cigarette into the food remaining on his plate. "As Petre said, the U.S. has many ways of pressuring our federal agents into interfering with our business. Some of the DEA SACs in Mexico City in the past have been reasonable men, willing to get rich and deflect some of that pressure." Drawing in another lung full of smoke, he let it trickle out of his mouth as he continued. "But not Hidalgo. He refuses our money. He is the worst kind of fool."

"And what kind is that?" Bolan asked.

"Honest," Jimenez said.

Bolan pushed his chair back and stood up. "I want to take a look at the DEA offices," he said, looking at Obregan. "I assume you'll be going with me."

Obregan nodded.

The Executioner turned back to Jimenez, who was still seated. "We'll take a look at the layout and unless there are some unforeseen interferences, I should be able to have him dead for you by tonight."

"Why not just kill the man at his home?" Jimenez asked. "It would be much easier."

The Executioner shook his head. "I'll shoot people," he said. "But I don't shoot men in front of their wives and children. Not if there's any other way to get the job done."

Jimenez nodded and, on his face, Bolan even saw an expression of approval.

"Now," the Executioner said. "There's one other thing I'm going to assume."

"And that is…?" Jimenez let the sentence trail off.

"That the fact that you or Obregan have to keep your eyes on me all the time doesn't include me going to the bathroom," Bolan said. "Which I have to do about this time every morning, in case you're keeping score."

Jimenez laughed as he stubbed what remained of his cigarette out on his plate. "I believe we can grant you that privacy," he said. "Petre, accompany Señor Mikhailovich to his room. But wait in the hallway for him."

Obregan got up from the table, followed Bolan out of the kitchen into the hall, then down the hall and up the steps. He stopped, as instructed, just outside the door of the guest room, folding his arms and leaning back against the wall.

The Executioner closed the bedroom door behind him, walked into the bathroom, and closed and locked that door, too. Then, stepping into the shower, he slid the opaque plastic door along its track as quietly as possible. Pulling the Texas quarter radio from his pocket, he pressed the inscriptions on its face, then stuck the coin in his ear.

A second later, Jack Grimaldi was saying, "Come in, Striker."

"Can you hear me?" Bolan whispered.

"Just barely," Grimaldi said. "Sounds like you're at the bottom of a well."

"No," the Executioner said quietly. "Just a shower. I've got curious ears just outside in the hall, so this is as loud as it's going to get."

"Okay, big guy," Grimaldi said. "Like I said, it's good enough—barely. What's up?"

Quickly, and with as few words as possible, Bolan ran the situation down to the pilot. "I need you to tell all of this to Brognola," he finally said.

"No problem," Grimaldi told him. "Hal's at the Justice Department right now. I just talked to him about some of this other stuff."

"What other stuff?" the Executioner asked.

"Yeah," Grimaldi said. "I keep forgetting you're out of pocket as to the mainstream news in the States. This New Symbionese Liberation Army thing. They kidnapped the daughter of a rich Texas oilman last night and they're demanding ten billion dollars ransom. That, and the fact that some of the local and campus police departments around the country are gearing up for peace demonstrations this weekend. I swear, sometimes I think we're back to living in the sixties again."

"Okay," Bolan said. "Now, here's what else I want you to tell Hal." He went on to repeat the plan he'd come up with between the time Jimenez had told him he wanted George Hidalgo killed and the present. "Hal can tell the DEA I'm a Justice agent who needs to maintain his cover," he finished.

At the other end of the airwaves, Bolan heard Grimaldi whistle. "What's *that* mean, Jack?" he asked.

"It means you're cutting things a little thin, don't you think?" the pilot answered. "What if this Obregan character decides to jump in and—"

"Jack, if you've got a better idea I'm more than willing to listen to it," the Executioner said.

"I don't," the pilot conceded. "But I can give you about a hundred and fifty potential scenarios where this one goes off track and the good guy gets killed instead of the bad."

"I don't think that'll happen," Bolan said, glancing at his watch. He'd been in the bathroom only a couple of minutes—Obregan would have no reason to be suspicious yet. "The way this goes down Hidalgo is a long way from the action."

"Hidalgo wasn't the good guy I was referring to," Grimaldi said. "The good guy I was talking about getting killed was *you*."

"All part of my job description," Bolan said. "Now, give Hal a call and get things rolling, will you?"

"I'm on it as soon as you hang up," the pilot said.

"Good. I'll get back to you later with the final details. In the mean time, make sure Hal tells everybody at the Mexico City DEA offices to go on about their normal routines. If we tip our hands too early, Jimenez will just come up with some other test for me."

"Got it, big guy. Over and out."

Bolan pulled the quarter from his ear and dropped it back into his pocket. Sliding the shower door quietly back again, he flushed the toilet, then turned the water on in the sink for several seconds, running his hands through the cold stream before drying them on a towel. They were still damp when he left the bathroom and crossed the bedroom to the hallway.

As soon as the Executioner stepped into the hall, Obregan extended his hand forward. It was a strange and awkward time for a handshake, and Bolan saw through the ruse even before he accepted the other man's hand.

"I just want to tell you," Obregan said. "That it is a pleasure working with a man of your skills."

The words were as thin as the handshake itself—almost to the point of being painful. What Obregan was really doing was checking to see if the Executioner had just washed his hands. It wasn't personal hygiene the gunman was concerned about, either. He suspected, with the animal cunning with which so many career criminals seemed to be born, that something beyond normal bodily functions had just gone down behind the closed doors.

Obregan didn't know what that something was, but he knew it was there.

"The pleasure is all mine," Bolan said in his Russian-accented Spanish, then dropped Obregan's hand.

Without another word, the two men walked down the stairs and out of the house.

14

Bolan stared out the window as Obregan guided the dirty blue-and-white Bronco down the wide avenue. Stretching between the heart of the old city and the Bosque Chapultepec park, by day Paseo del Reforma was one of the most beautiful areas in all of Mexico City. But as soon as darkness fell, the street would become the turf of prostitutes, pimps and drug dealers.

In addition to the government buildings Bolan noticed, there were other tall, modern structures, lining both sides of the wide roadway, with historic monuments marking important intersections in the center of the avenue. Large Mexican cities were always more alive with uniforms than their American counterparts, and hurrying down the sidewalks he saw men and women dressed in the distinctive designs of private companies as well as different branches of the Mexican government.

"The DEA offices are down this side street," Obregan said as he twisted the Bronco's steering wheel and they rounded a corner. "They make no secret about it." He coughed out a small laugh that sounded more like a grunt. "They have another office across town, however, which they think no one knows about. We watch it, too."

Obregan's words had been a statement and required no answer, so Bolan remained silent. The only part of what the gunman had just said that he had to question was that the DEA thought their second office was a secret. It was not uncommon for foreign offices of the DEA, CIA and other agencies who relied heavily on clandestine operations, to have *three* offices in the same town. One, like the one toward which he and Obregan were now headed, was "above cover" for the public. The second office, in Obregan's view "the one they thought no one knew about," was little more than a sham. Agents came and went furtively, but not so furtively that the criminal element didn't soon learn of its existence. Its sole purpose was to divert attention from the third office, which was where the real undercover agents gathered to plan and carry out their operations. Not even the police of the host country, some of whom could be trusted, others who couldn't, with the American agents never quite sure which were which, were aware of these third sites.

Obregan brought the Bronco to a halt at the first stoplight a block off Reforma. "The public office is located on the third floor on the next corner," he said. "Hidalgo drives a new Chevrolet Impala, which he parks in his privately marked spot in the parking lot to the side of the building. We will pass it." The light turned green and he drove through the intersection.

"Don't just pass it," the Executioner instructed his driver. "Find a place to pull in. I want to study the area."

Obregan blew air through his clenched teeth in mild disgust. "Why?" he asked as he followed a rickety flatbed truck down the street. "I have told you everything you need to know. As Jimenez said, George Hidalgo no longer hides his identity and he has become a true bureaucrat, a creature of habit." The gunman looked down at his wristwatch. "It is after nine. He is inside, at his desk."

"Which door does he use?" Bolan asked.

By now they were passing the corner and Obregan used his peculiar two-finger point to indicate the front of the building. "That front one," he said.

"Where does he park his car?" the Executioner asked.

"I told you," the gunner said. "He has his own marked space in the parking lot...right there." He jabbed his fingers again as they passed the lot. "It is that corner space, closest to the front door." He paused to draw in a breath. "As you see, the driver's side faces us." As they drove on past he finished with, "If I were you, I would just wait farther back in the parking lot, walk up to him as he gets in or out of the car and put a bullet in his back."

"I don't doubt that you would," the Executioner said. "And you'd be likely to get shot yourself in return. Or at least wind up in jail." He paused a moment to let the insult set in, then added, "But I'm not you, Obregan. I'll do this my way or not at all." As soon as he'd finished speaking silence fell over the Bronco.

Bolan had noted that Obregan's hostility toward him had been steadily increasing as they continued to work together. And he knew its source: jealousy, pure and simple. Maybe Obregan was worried that Fernando Jimenez would replace him with Anton Mikhailovich. The Executioner reminded himself to watch his back as well as his front when Obregan was around.

The Executioner spotted a parking lot across from the one servicing the DEA building, and directed Obregan to pull in. As soon as they had paid the attendant, the Executioner said, "Find us a spot facing where Hidalgo parks."

Obregan did so, then twisted the key, killing the engine. Using his two pointing fingers again, he tapped the windshield toward the side of the DEA building. "You see the Impala on the end?" he asked.

"I see it."

"That's his." Again, the Jimenez gunman looked at his watch. "But he will not come out for nearly two and a half more hours."

"Good," the Executioner said. He stuck his head out the window, glancing around at the neighboring buildings. The one just behind the lot where they had parked was a four-story edifice with a flat roof. It would do nicely for what he had in mind.

Pulling his head back into the car, the Executioner hooked a thumb over his shoulder. "What building is that?" he asked.

"I do not know the name," Obregan said, raising one eyebrow in curiosity. "But it is another office building. Several companies are located there. The bottom floor is a bank." He stopped speaking for a second, then added, "Why do you ask?"

"Because we're going to make good use of it," said the Executioner. He checked his own watch, then said, "Let's go."

"Go?" Obregan questioned. "Go where? We—you—came to shoot the man. All we have to do is wait until noon."

Bolan shook his head. "I told you it's my way or no way," he said. "Start the engine and drive back to the hacienda. With luck, we'll be back by the time he leaves for lunch. If not, we'll get him when he comes back for the afternoon shift."

Again, Obregan showed his disgust, this time with a scowl on his face. "You are making something simple into something difficult," he muttered as he twisted the key in the ignition and backed out of the parking space. "The American agents are not even allowed to carry guns in Mexico."

Bolan let out a laugh. "Don't kid yourself, Petre," he said. "You and I aren't supposed to be carrying guns, either."

Another unintelligible grunt issued from Obregan's clenched lips.

"I don't know exactly how it works with your government agents down here," Bolan said as they left the parking lot and started back down Paseo de Reforma, "but I can tell you how it works in Russia and the United States." He waited for a second while Obregan shot him a quick glance, then began speaking again when the gunner had turned his attention back to the street. "You kill a Russian or American cop," Bolan went on, "and every other cop in the country feels like they just lost a brother. And this is an American cop I'm getting ready to kill, which means the DEA, FBI and every other American Fed stationed in Mexico or anywhere else is going to put a sudden stop on whatever they're doing and go looking for the shooter. I plan to be way out of the picture when that happens."

Obregan had listened, and by the expression on his face Bolan knew the man realized he was right. But his being right about anything didn't sit well with Jimenez's number two man, and his face fell into a bitter sulk as they retraced their path down Reforma.

Forty-five minutes later they had returned to the affluent suburb and were pulling the Bronco into the circular drive-way leading to the hacienda. Obregan used the remote control to open the garage door, and they entered the house the same way they had left. As they passed an open door inside the garage, Bolan happened to glance into the storage closet. Passing over the mops, brooms, hand and garden tools, and other items hanging from the walls and stacked on metal shelves, his eyes fell on some paint cans and soiled coveralls.

Fernando Jimenez had retired to the swimming pool area in the central courtyard and lay back on a padded chair, reading a newspaper. Dressed in nothing but swim trunks, he looked up in surprise when he saw Bolan and Obregan come out of the house to join him.

"You are already finished?" he asked, glancing at his wristwatch.

Bolan shook his head. "No." This was a simple reconnaissance mission. I needed to see the layout. But I now know how to do it, and I'll keep my promise and have him dead for you before the day's over. I'll need a few things, however."

"As the Bible tells us," Jimenez said, "ask, and ye shall receive."

Bolan nodded. "Most of what I need I saw in the maintenance closet in the garage," he said. "But I also need a good rifle with a scope, and one that's already zeroed in because I don't have time to do it myself. It's not going to be a particularly difficult shot, and it doesn't have to be a heavy caliber. But it's got to be able to hit its mark from seventy-five to a hundred yards."

Jimenez was on his feet, dropping the newspaper onto the recliner behind him. "Follow me," he said, and started for the house.

Bolan and Obregan fell in behind him.

Jimenez led them through the sliding glass doors facing the courtyard to a staircase at the rear of the hacienda. They descended into a basement where the house's central heat and air system, water tank and other utility bases were located. Then Jimenez walked to a set of cabinets against the wall. But instead of opening any of the cabinet doors, he turned to what appeared to be a barometer hung on the side wall, reached up and wrapped his hand around the circular device.

Turning to the Executioner, he smiled and said, "You are about to learn yet another of my secrets, my friend Anton. Perhaps I am actually beginning to trust you after all."

Bolan returned the smile. "It's about time," he said good-naturedly. "After Hidalgo is dead, I hope we can quit playing silly games and make some money."

Jimenez didn't answer. Turning back to the barometer, he twisted it clockwise and the cabinets in front of them began to revolve. When they had disappeared on the other side of the wall, the Executioner saw an array of firearms and ammunition that could have outfitted a Third World army. Stacked at one end of the wall was a collection of OD green metal ammo boxes that were labeled to contain every caliber of military cartridge imaginable. The rest of the wall held rack after rack of handguns, shotguns, submachine guns and rifles.

What the Executioner was interested in at the moment were the scoped bolt-actions.

Jimenez had figured out that his guest planned a sniping attack rather than a close-quarter engagement. "You may choose whatever you like, of course," he said. "But I must tell you, my personal preference for what it seems as if you are planning would be this Winchester." He reached out and lifted a 30-06 with a Simmons scope from the rack, then handed it to the Executioner. He explained the sighting.

Bolan took the rifle and looked it over. "Sounds perfect," he said. "You're sure about the sighting?"

Jimenez nodded. "I have not fired it for six months or so. But it has rested safely here ever since so there is little chance that the scope has shifted." He reached behind the rifles and pulled out a box of twenty 30-06 soft points. "This is the ammunition with which it was sighted. Will you need more than one box?"

Bolan shook his head. "If I do, I'll be dead before I could reload anyway," he said.

The statement amused Jimenez and he laughed out loud. "I like the way you think," he said. Then, again looking at his watch, he said, "When will you do this exactly?"

Consulting his own timepiece, the Executioner said, "I doubt that we can get back before he leaves for lunch. But we should have plenty of time to set up and be ready when he comes back to the office at one."

"Good." Jimenez nodded. "Very good. Then I will see you

when you return. And if you are successful, we will begin talking about our new business relationship." He reached to a shelf above the rifle racks, pulled down a cased spotter's scope and handed it to Obregan. "Here, Petre," he said. "Make yourself useful."

The comment drew a frown from the number two man. It was confirmation that Bolan was in charge—at least on this mission.

Jimenez twisted the barometer the other way and the rifles and other guns disappeared as the cabinets rotated back into view. Bolan and Obregan followed the man back up the stairs. Then, after a quick handshake, Jimenez headed back out to the swimming pool.

Bolan, carrying the Winchester 30-06, and Obregan with the spotter's scope, started back through the house toward the garage. Near the door leading out, the Executioner noticed a small rest room. They walked through the door toward the Bronco but instead of going directly to the vehicle, the Executioner led the gunman into the maintenance closet. Grabbing two pairs of coveralls, brushes, a heavily spotted drop cloth and a gallon can of paint, they toted the equipment to the car and stowed it in the back seat.

"I'll be with you in a minute," Bolan told Obregan as the man slid behind the wheel. "But before we go I've got to take a leak." The Mexican's face showed the same look of suspicion that had been there earlier.

"What's wrong with you, Mikhailovich?" Obregan said. "Do you have the clap or something?"

Bolan forced a chuckle. "Not that I know of," he said.

"Small bladder, I guess." Without waiting for a reply he walked back through the garage, into the house and into the small rest room.

With the door closed behind him, the Executioner waited a full sixty seconds, his ear pressed against the hollow-core wood to see if Obregan had followed him inside. This rest room didn't allow for the privacy the other had, and he suspected that even if he kept his voice low it might be heard outside.

When he was finally convinced that Obregan had stayed in the Bronco, the Executioner pulled out the Texas quarter radio and contacted Grimaldi. "Hal talked to the DEA?" he asked the pilot.

"Affirmative," Grimaldi came back. "And the DEA Washington office has talked to Hidalgo. Like you suggested, he's been told you're a Justice agent caught in a tight spot and trying to keep your cover intact."

"That's exactly what I am, Jack," Bolan said. "If you leave out the Justice agent part."

"Right," Grimaldi agreed. "In any case, Hidalgo is willing to go along with it, no questions asked."

"Hal pulls a lot of weight."

"Yes, he does." Grimaldi paused a second, then said, "I assume you're calling to finalize the details?"

"I am. I'll be shooting from the roof of a four-story building across from the DEA office. Both Obregan and I will be dressed in painter's coveralls. The cue for my first shot will be when Hidalgo gets out of his car. Tell him to make sure he drops his keys and bends over to pick them up. All in one smooth motion."

Through the quarter stuck in his ear, the Executioner heard Grimaldi laugh. "That's the only part Hidalgo was a little hinky about," the pilot said. "A guy he's never even met shooting just over his head. Hal had to assure him you're an expert shot."

"I can't blame Hidalgo for worrying about it," Bolan said. "It's asking a lot of any man. But if he's scared now, wait until it's over. I've got to come within a gnat's hair of hitting him to make it look real."

"You'll do it," Grimaldi said. "That's still not the part that worries me."

"Don't waste your time worrying," the Executioner said. "Whatever's meant to happen will happen."

"You realize the other DEA agents involved in this deal don't know you any better than Hidalgo does? And with both you and this Obregan character dressed alike—"

"Just remind them I'll be the tall gringo," Bolan interrupted. "And make sure they know I need Obregan alive."

"They aren't real crazy about that part, either," Grimaldi said. "Boy, talk about taking one for the team...." He let his voice trail off, then came back with, "But you be careful. There's still a good chance of them panicking, forgetting the plan, and making a false ID. I'd just hate to see you get killed by friendly fire, is all."

Bolan brushed off the statement. "What's new on your end?" he asked.

"Nothing except more about this New Symbionese Liberation Army," Grimaldi said. "They've still got Sue Ellen Waters hidden somewhere. And they're demanding two million bucks to the American Communist Party as an act of good faith on the part of her father, J. Travis Waters."

Bolan knew Waters was one of the wealthiest men in America, a Texas oil magnate. "I'd have thought it would have been more," he said.

"Oh, it is," Grimaldi said. "It is. Like I said, the two million is just an act of good faith." The pilot stopped to take a deep breath, then said, "In addition to that, they want—get this—ten billion dollars for her safe return."

The Executioner felt his jaw tighten grimly. "That means they don't plan to return her," he said. "Not even Waters can come up with that kind of cash. At least not fast enough to save her."

Grimaldi agreed, then said, "Evidently that's what the old man told them himself. They called his house yesterday to make their demands."

"FBI get a trace?" Bolan asked.

"Sure did." Grimaldi laughed sarcastically. "Some place in Tanzania."

Bolan felt his eyebrows lower. Aaron Kurtzman was one of the best computer and electronics men in the world. But it didn't take the best to reroute area codes and phone numbers, and it sounded as if this New Symbionese Liberation Army had somebody who was at least competent enough for that.

"They also sent a letter to *The New York Times*," Grimaldi went on without prompting. "One of those things where all of the letters were cut out of magazines. The *Times* not only printed the context, they photographed it and printed it, crazy lettering and all. It got picked up by all of the wire services. It was signed by some screwball calling himself Field Marshal Pentad."

Bolan felt both of his hands tighten into fists. He had heard that name—Pentad—somewhere recently. Where? He couldn't remember. But he'd have time to mull it over in his unconscious mind while he got ready for the sniper operation on George Hidalgo. "Anything else?" he asked Grimaldi.

"Just good luck," the pilot said. "And I'll see you when I see you. Assuming, that is, that I *do* see you again."

"You will," Bolan said firmly. Then, pulling the tiny radio from his ear, he dropped it into his pocket with the rest of his change and left the hacienda.

Obregan was behind the wheel when he got back into the Bronco.

"Are you finally ready?" the Jimenez gunman asked impatiently.

Bolan nodded his head and gave the man a wide smile. "Let's go," he said. "We'll pull the coveralls on at a gas station along the way."

AS OBREGAN HAD SAID, the Bank of Mexico took up the first floor of what turned out to be the Rodriguez Building. Through the windows as they approached, Bolan could see both male and female employees dressed smartly in blue blazers and gray slacks or skirts.

Holding the outer door for Obregan with one hand, the Winchester 30-06 wrapped in the drop cloth with the other, the Executioner waited for the Jimenez gunman to walk past him, then followed the man to the stairs just outside the bank proper. This time it was Obregan who held the door, clutching a variety of paint brushes, the cased spotter's scope, and the can of paint under his other arm. No one in the bank gave them a second glance as the door to the stairwell swung shut behind them.

"This is a lot of trouble," Obregan said as they started up the steps. "For a job as simple as killing a man."

"Keep your voice down," the Executioner cautioned. "You never know who might be listening."

The Jimenez gunman was out of shape and breathing hard by the time they mounted the steps beyond the fourth floor and opened the door to the roof. Bolan maneuvered his way through a variety of ventilator posts and retaining wires to the side of the building that faced the DEA's Mexico City office. As he reached the edge, he stayed on his feet only long enough to get an eyeful of the empty parking space across the street and below, implanting into his brain a visual image of the spot where George Hidalgo's Chevrolet Impala would soon park. Then he dropped down out of view behind the short retaining wall.

Neither man spoke as the Executioner began slowly unwrapping the drop cloth from around the 30-06. He looked at his watch.

The hands read 12:38.

"We've got roughly twenty minutes to wait," Obregan said bitterly after looking at his own wrist.

The Executioner pointed to the paint can the man had carried up the steps. "You're welcome to do a little painting to pass the time if you'd like," he said.

The Jimenez man grunted.

Bolan took advantage of the time to concentrate; closing

his eyes, regulating his breathing, and making sure he was in the right frame of mind for the split-second timing his plan would require. He wanted his complete attention focused on the task before him. Any mistake on his part—however small—could mean that one or more of the DEA agents stationed in Mexico City lost their lives.

As Grimaldi had noted, the plan had about a thousand different ways in which to go wrong once the shooting started.

The Executioner opened his eyes to see Obregan staring at him. The Mexican gunman looked away. Bolan reached to his side and drew the Desert Eagle, dropping the magazine to make sure it was loaded, then pulling the slide back far enough to see that a round was already chambered. Pushing the safety back on with his thumb, he repeated the process with the Beretta. With the Desert Eagle, it had been nothing but a show for Obregan's benefit. Bolan had no intention of using the big gun. But the Beretta, filled with the same low-velocity subsonic rounds he usually carried to work in conjunction with the sound suppressor, would play a vital role in the drama about to unfold.

Bolan looked at his watch again: 12:55.

Lifting the bolt-action Winchester, the Executioner fed three of the long .30 caliber soft points into the magazine, racked the bolt back and chambered the first. He looked up as Obregan unzipped the tubular case and pulled out the spotter's scope. "Go ahead and set up the scope," the Executioner told the man. "If he's as much a creature of habit as you say, he'll be here in another five minutes."

"He *is* what I say he is," Obregan said huffily. "And tell me—exactly when did I start taking orders from you?"

It was the first openly resentful thing Obregan had said, and it seemed to embarrass him that he'd suddenly revealed his jealousy. Almost as soon as the words had left his mouth he looked to the side, avoiding Bolan's eyes again.

But the Executioner kept his eyes on Obregan as the man pulled the legs out beneath the spotter's scope and set it over his head on the retaining wall. The Jimenez syndicate man was going to play a more important role than he knew. Rather than go through with the elaborate hoax the Executioner was orchestrating, it would have been easier to just kill Petre Obregan himself, then tell Jimenez the DEA had done it after his own shots with the 30-06 had missed Hidalgo. But a story like that wouldn't carry near the weight coming from Bolan that it would from Obregan.

The Executioner waited until his spotter had risen to his knees behind the scope, then said, "Okay. Now, if you don't mind, tell me as soon as you see his car. I don't want the rifle in view any longer than necessary."

Obregan nodded.

Bolan looked down at his watch and saw that it was now two minutes until one. At almost the same time, Obregan said, "Here he comes. He's a block away. To our right."

The 30-06 in both fists, the Executioner rose over the retaining wall suddenly, resting his forearms on the ledge. As he did so, he saw the Impala pull into the parking lot below and head for the empty space on the corner.

Along both sides of the street, men and women hurried back to their offices after lunch. The steady buzz of chatting voices drifted up to where Bolan and Obregan hid.

Bolan waited patiently as the Impala pulled to a halt and the door opened. First a leg wearing black shoes and charcoal slacks, then a torso in a matching suit coat, and finally a tanned face wearing sunglasses came out of the opening.

The Executioner took a deep breath and let half of it out.

George Hidalgo slammed the Chevy's door behind him, took a step away from the vehicle, then turned back to it, the remote-control locking device pointed toward the door. He stood now in almost perfect profile to the Executioner.

Bolan centered the scope on the spot of gray in Hidalgo's otherwise black hair. His index finger took up the slack in the trigger.

Suddenly, the keys fell from Hidalgo's fingers and the man lurched forward. At the same time, the 30-06 exploded in the Executioner's hands. The bullet skimmed across the back the DEA SAC's head, scorching his hair.

On the ground, the people along the sidewalks froze in place. Some looked up, some looked down, and others looked in every other possible direction. Finally, the first scream sounded as the roar of the big rifle died down. It was joined by a dozen more as the pedestrians thawed and scurried for cover.

"You missed him!" Obregan shouted from behind the scope. "Shoot again!"

Bolan worked the Winchester's bolt, racking the empty brass casing out of the weapon and chambering another round. He dropped the scope slightly, letting the crosshairs fall this time on the squatting Hidalgo's chest. Silently, he prayed that the man would follow his orders as precisely as they'd been given to him, then triggered the weapon once again.

The 30-06 sailed a fraction of an inch behind the DEA agent's back as Hidalgo rolled under the Impala. But for a brief moment, red and blue sparks scampered across the concrete where the Executioner's target had been a microsecond earlier.

"You missed again!" Obregan yelled, and his voice somehow conveyed both disgust and joy. In a slightly lower tone, he said, "He's under the car now! Let's go!" Jumping to his feet, the Jimenez gunman began ripping off his paint-spotted coveralls.

Bolan dropped the Winchester and stood too, taking a second to glance down at the street. The second shot had given away their position, and now every head that hadn't found cover stared up at him.

Including three men in suits similar to the one George Hidalgo had worn. With nearly identical sunglasses.

As Bolan ripped open his own coveralls, he saw the three men exit a car in the parking lot near the street, then sprint through the stalled traffic toward the Bank of Mexico below him.

By the time he caught up to Obregan the Executioner had shed his coveralls and was down to his street clothes. Obregan opened the door and raced through to the stairs, Bolan at his heels. The Jimenez man led the way down the steps, huffing and puffing from both excitement and exertion as they descended into the stairwell.

"You missed!" he managed to breathe out again as they reached the landing to the third floor.

Bolan didn't bother answering—just pushed Obregan on, drawing the Beretta as soon as the man was moving again.

Two seconds later, as they reached the bottom steps to the second floor, one of the men who had raced across the street from the parking lot burst through the doorway below them holding a Sig-Sauer .40-caliber pistol.

"Down!" Bolan shouted, and Obregan hit the landing on his chest.

The Executioner triggered a 3-round burst that hit the DEA agent squarely in the chest. The man dropped his gun and flew back against the wall of the stairwell. Bolan pulled Obregan to his feet and pushed him on as they made their way on down the steps to the ground floor. When Obregan tried to slow down in order to draw his own gun, the Executioner pushed him again, shouting, "No time! I've got us covered!"

The other two DEA agents appeared in the doorway just outside the bank as Bolan and Obregan reached the ground level. They held pistols identical to the one that had just clattered to the floor above them, and they tried to bring them up into play as soon as they saw the escaping men.

Bolan triggered another 3-round burst of fire, all three 147-grain 9 mm rounds striking the DEA agent on the left within an inch of one another.

Swinging the Beretta to his right, Bolan pulled the trigger again and another trio of 9 mm rounds exploded into the chest of the other DEA man.

Climbing over the sprawling bodies of the DEA men, Bolan and Obregan raced out onto the sidewalk. The Executioner hid the Beretta under his jacket as he ran after the man, sprinting down the street toward where they had left the Bronco parked, two blocks down. With everyone else on the sidewalks still screaming and hiding, the sudden appearance of two more running men drew no more attention than a green traffic light.

A block from the Bronco, Bolan reached out and grabbed Obregan's shoulder and they slowed to a walk. This far away from the action, the people on the street appeared more curious than frightened. As Obregan caught his breath again, they walked on to their vehicle and got inside.

Obregan took a deep breath, then shoved the keys into the Bronco and started the engine. As the vehicle roared to life, he pulled out of the parking lot and onto the street. Without a word to the Executioner, he drew a cell phone from his inside jacket pocket and tapped in a series of numbers. A moment later, the Executioner heard him say, "He missed Hidalgo," into the instrument.

There was a pause of several seconds while the man on the other end of the call—it could be no one but Fernando Jimenez—spoke. Then Obregan shook his head rapidly back and forth as if he thought his employer could see the gesture. "No," he said. "It was just bad luck." The Jimenez gunman paused for another gulp of oxygen as he stopped for a red light, then said, "He killed three other DEA agents as we escaped."

Bolan was tempted to let out a sigh of relief but resisted the urge. Good. With everything else going on, the fact that the DEA agents were wearing bullet-resistant vests had gone unnoticed by the Jimenez man.

There was another pause, then Obregan ended the call and dropped the phone back in his pocket.

Turning to the Executioner, he said, "We are to return to the hacienda."

Bolan nodded, then sat back against the seat for the ride. What had looked like a bungled sniping to Obregan had actually been an operation that had gone off without a flaw, and the Executioner had to fight to keep the relief off his face as he thought of it. The DEA men—from Special Agent in Charge Hidalgo on down to the three street agents who had confronted them on their way out of the building—had played their parts perfectly.

They would have very sore and bruised chests beneath the Kevlar and iron. But other than that, all three men would be just fine.

The light turned from red to green and Obregan pulled out into the intersection as police sirens began wailing in the distance. The Bronco was traveling away from the scene of the shootings so the sirens grew quieter, rather than louder, as they drove. It was a rare experience for the Executioner, who was far more accustomed to leaving the scene a split second before the authorities arrived, and he was reminded of one definition of the difference between warriors and other men.

Most men ran away from gunfire when they heard it.

Warriors ran toward it.

FERNANDO JIMENEZ WAS still wearing his swim trunks and sitting by the side of the pool when Bolan and Obregan returned to the hacienda. He lifted a tall coffee mug in salute as they stepped out of the plant-stuffed conservatory leading to the courtyard, then took a sip from it as they walked around the swimming pool. A thin line of what looked like whipped cream covered his upper lip when he had finished, and he wiped it away with a forearm, then dried the arm on his trunks.

"It sounds as if you encountered some unforseen obstacle," the front man for the Jimenez organization said, smacking his lips. "Latte?" He reached for the bell at his side but frowned when he saw the look on Bolan's and Obregan's faces. With the bell still held in midair, he said, "No?"

Both Obregan and the Executioner stopped directly in front of the man. Bolan waited for Obregan to speak. Jimenez's head henchman's account of the "mishap" would carry far more weight than his own.

"As I told you on the phone," Obregan said. "He missed. Hidalgo is still alive." He glanced to his side at the Executioner. Then, grudgingly, as if having to force the words from his very heart, he added, "But it was not Mikhailovich's fault." He fell silent again, his face looking as if he had just bitten down on a piece of rotten fruit.

Jimenez set his cup and the bell on the table next to him. "Perhaps you should explain further, Petre," he said.

Obregan looked down at the concrete beneath his feet for a moment. Then, again grimacing as if the words he spoke tasted bad, he said, "It was simply bad luck. The plan was to shoot Hidalgo when he got out of his car after lunch." He glanced quickly toward the Executioner, then went on. "At the very second Mikhailovich pulled the trigger, the man dropped his keys and bent forward to retrieve them." The Jimenez gunman pantomimed Hidalgo's actions for his boss's benefit, then added, "I saw the bullet cut through the man's hair with my own eyes—through the spotter's scope."

Jimenez had been watching his second in command during the speech. But now he turned toward Bolan, looking deeply into his eyes.

Obregan answered the unasked question. "No," he said. "It was far too close to be faked. No man alive could have come that close without actually killing his target." He stopped for a quick breath, then said, "And the follow-up shot—just before Hidalgo rolled to cover beneath his vehicle—was just as close." Now Obregan, too, turned to face the Executioner. "And during our escape, I watched him shoot three other DEA agents."

"You saw them die?" Jimenez asked, taking another sip of his latte.

Obregan snorted. "We were not in a position to wait around for such entertainment," he said. "But they could not have lived. All three were hit squarely in the chest and went down hard."

Jimenez's face brightened. "Well, Anton," he said. "Or perhaps I should say my good friend Anton instead. It appears you are indeed to be trusted. You are who you say you are— a Russian-born naturalized American citizen who is also a criminal." He laughed at his words and waited for the Executioner's response.

"I'm glad you finally understand that," Bolan said simply. "Now, do you suppose we can get down to business?"

"All in good time," Jimenez said. "You and I will definitely do business," he said. "And there will be no need to begin with low return nonsense such as illegal immigration.

We will start immediately with cocaine, heroin and top-end marijuana. But first, now that we are partners, there is something I would ask of you." He saw the Executioner's facial expression and shook his head quickly. "No, not another test. It is more of a…favor."

Bolan waited.

"Tomorrow night," Jimenez said, "I have a most lucrative deal going down on the American border. So lucrative, in fact, that I have set up several other drug deals to coincide with it and divert the attention of both the Americans and federal agents." He glanced quickly to the man at Bolan's side, then said, "I would like you and Obregan to supervise the transaction."

Bolan blew air through his clenched teeth to show impatience. "You may call it a favor," he said, "but it sounds an awful lot like another test to me."

Jimenez shook his head. "No, my friend," he said. "It is not. We will indeed become fifty-fifty partners in everything I send through Florida. But I need a man with your firearms skill in order to feel comfortable about the transaction tomorrow night. We are dealing with a group that is…" He paused for moment, frowning as he searched for the correct words. "Unstable," he finally said. "I have sold them many drugs in the past. But they are not businessmen such as us. The fact is, they are led by a man who is quite insane in my opinion."

The Executioner returned the frown as a thought suddenly surfaced. Even before he understood it fully he said, "You are speaking of Pentad."

Jimenez had been about to speak again, but the word

caused him to stop with his mouth still open. Several seconds passed, then he said, "How did you know that?"

Bolan shrugged, remembering the first night of this mission when the preppie-clad drug dealers had fought it out with Sanchez and his men. They had both joked about their head men coming to such a transaction in person. And the name the Mexicans had used when referring to the American leader had been Pentad. "I read the newspapers," the Executioner said. "And in Russia as well as America, two plus two equals four." He saw a smile begin to creep over Jimenez's face and returned it. "I assume the math is the same in Mexico."

Jimenez burst out in laughter. Turning to Obregan, he said, "Ah, Petre! You could learn much from this man!"

It did not appear to have been said as an insult but Obregan could take it no other way. The gunman bristled, and Bolan reminded himself of the man's jealousy and the fact that Obregan might turn on him at any time. "This sounds like something Petre could handle for you," Bolan said, purposefully using the man's first name. "He's as good as I am—he's just been holding back in order to let me prove myself." In his peripheral vision, he saw the gunman relax slightly.

Jimenez seemed to suddenly sense that he had offended his lieutenant and looked again to Obregan. "Yes, yes, yes," he said. "I did not wish to criticize you, Petre. But in the same sense that 'two heads are better than one,' I believe that two gunmen, backed up by other of our men of course, would be superior to only one man I can fully trust."

"No offense was taken," Obregan said, which was obviously a lie.

Ignoring the psychological play going on between the other two men, Bolan forced another sigh of impatience from his clenched lips. "Okay," he said. "I'll go on this deal with Obregan. But now that we're business partners, and I'm no longer proving myself, I'm going to have to demand some remuneration for risking my life for you."

"I would expect no less," Jimenez said. "This job will pay you one hundred thousand U.S. dollars."

"No," Bolan said. "It'll pay me one-fifty thousand U.S. American dollars. And I'll split it fifty-fifty with Obregan as a bonus for action above and beyond the call of duty as they say." Out of the corner of his eye, he watched the confused emotions of hatred, jealousy, and greed fight for control of Obregan's face.

That was fine with the Executioner; he wasn't trying to win the man over. He just wanted to keep him off balance.

Jimenez laughed again. "It will be as you wish, my partner," he said. "But do not ask for more because you will not get it." He stood up, stretched his arms over his head, and sat back down again.

"I think you'd better tell us a little more about this deal," Bolan said. "The way you phrased things, it doesn't sound like drugs we'll be delivering."

Jimenez shook his head. "It isn't," he said. "What you will be taking to the demented man who calls himself Field Marshal Pentad will be VX nerve gas."

A long and very poignant pause followed the statement. Bolan finally broke the silence with, "Where in the world did you come up with that?" He made the question come off sounding as if he were simply amazed, rather than seeking more intelligence information.

And that was how Jimenez took it. Shrugging, the front man said, "It is my understanding that it is Soviet surplus that fell into other hands during the confusion of the early nineties," he said. "In any case, it is disguised as crowd control pepper-spray canisters. I cannot read the labels but—" he stopped speaking as a sudden thought occurred to him, then finished the sentence with "—but you could. Would you like to see them?"

Bolan nodded. "If I'm going to be delivering them, I want to know ahead of time exactly what I've got."

Without another word Jimenez got up from his recliner and led Bolan and Obregan back into the house, then down into the basement where the revolving wall hid the firearms arsenal. Once again manipulating the phony barometer, the cabinets twirled out of sight and the guns appeared.

Jimenez leaned down and lifted a metal ammunition box from the stack Bolan had seen earlier. He set it, and the one under it, on the floor, then flipped the catch on the third box down and opened the lid. "I have been wondering at the labels," Jimenez said as he stepped back to let Bolan move in.

The Executioner reached down and pulled a large round canister from the ammo box, noting that two more identical cans were below it. Lifting it up into the light, he read the Russian label and translated it into Spanish. "It says exactly what you said it is," he said. "It's a crowd control pepper-spray device. You set it on the ground, flip the switch and it begins to revolve and shoot out pepper spray."

"Except," said Jimenez, smiling slyly, "regardless of what the label says, these specific canisters will shoot out VX nerve gas instead."

Bolan replaced the can in the box and closed the lid. "I don't really understand," he said. "These cans are going to kill whoever activates them as well as everyone else around. Is this Pentad guy planning on rigging up some remote-control trigger?"

Jimenez pushed his closed lips out in an almost kissing motion and shrugged his shoulders. "Who knows?" he said. "And who cares? Once he has paid me I do not care what he does with them."

Bolan nodded in agreement. "Just business," he said, and lifted the metal ammo box off the stack.

"Just business," Jimenez agreed. "Now, it is time for you and Obregan to depart for the border. It has been my pleasure having you as my guest, and I look forward to your return. *With* the two million dollars you receive for the canisters, of course."

"Of course," the Executioner said. "And I tell you what. Since you were kind enough to up my cut on this deal, we'll take my plane and pilot. No charge."

Jimenez laughed. "You are a true professional," he said and stuck out his hand. "Petre knows the details of the transfer, and he can fill you in on the way."

Bolan shifted the ammo box handle to his left hand and took the front man's hand with his right. As they shook hands, the Executioner looked into the other man's eyes. While Jimenez exhibited a great deal of emotion on the outside, the orbs set in his head were dead. He had summed up his sociopathic personality with two simple words when referring to what Kauffman would do with the VX: "Who cares?"

The two men were still shaking hands as Jimenez said, "I have already reserved a hotel room for you in Nuevo Laredo, near the area where the sale will take place. Several men from Pentad's group have met Obregan before. They will recognize his face, and nothing should go wrong. But two of my local men will meet you at the hotel and go along to back you up. Just in case."

Bolan nodded his understanding, then dropped Jimenez's hand. Silently, he vowed that the next time he raised his own hand toward the syndicate front man, he would have a gun in it.

Then he led Obregan up the stairs and out of the house.

15

"Much different kind of bank job we're pulling this time, Field Marshal," Delbert Washington said as he got out of the driver's seat of the van.

"Yes, indeed," Kauffman said as he exited the passenger door. "Nice, quiet, and almost legal." He glanced quickly up and down the street as the two men strolled casually across the parking lot of the First National Bank of New Braunfels. A variety of businesses, including a German restaurant and a German-oriented curio shop, lined the sidewalks. Germans, Kauffman thought. Perhaps even some of my ancestors. A sudden sense of shame flooded his soul as the fact sunk in. People just like him had settled this country.

They could have made it great. But, instead, they had become greedy capitalist pigs.

Kauffman forced himself to smile as they reached the front door. At least he was about to redistribute some of the ill-gotten gains. Unconsciously, he patted the Glock 21 .45-caliber pistol stuck in his belt just behind his hip. Both he and Washington were carrying Glocks, just in case. But if everything went according to plan, the guns wouldn't be needed.

Washington reached for the door handle, but Kauffman lunged past him. Swinging the door back, he waved to his second in command to enter first. Even though they were both dressed in subdued gray business suits and playing the parts of wealthy conventional men, he could not bear the thought of someone seeing a black man open the door for him. It simply wouldn't look right.

Walking past a cash machine in the entryway, Kauffman raced on to get the door to the bank lobby as well. He thought he saw a thin smile of amusement cross Washington's lips as the man stopped and waited for the door, then walked through first again. Kauffman followed, letting the door swing shut behind him.

Bank President Charles Delano saw them come in through the glass wall of his office and was on his feet immediately. The jacket to his navy blue suit hung over the back of his chair but he grabbed it and stuck his pudgy arms into the sleeves as he made his way to them, his belly threatening to burst the buttons from the front of his white shirt. "Ah, Mr. Kauffman," Delano said. "How good to see you again."

Turning toward Washington, he said, "And you must be Mr.—"

"Carver," Washington said, taking the hand in his. "John Jefferson Carver."

"Carver?" Delano said, raising his eyebrows. "I can't help but ask. Are you any relation to the great African-American—"

"No," Washington said, and Kauffman could see that his grin was at the white man's awkwardness.

"Shall we go into my office?" Delano asked. Without waiting for an answer, he turned on his heels and led them inside.

Kauffman looked at his watch as they took seats across from the bank president's desk. He had called the Waters home again, instructing J. Travis that he would call at exactly 1330 hours to give him the account number where the two million dollars was to be wired. By now, he knew, the FBI would have determined that the American Communist Party not only had nothing to do with this wire transfer, they were not involved with the New Symbionese Liberation Army in any way. But it no longer mattered. Kauffman had made it clear that Waters would have one chance, and one chance only, to keep his daughter alive. And that chance hinged on his ability to write down the account number and complete the transfer within sixty seconds of the call.

If all went well, Field Marshal Pentad and Colonel Washington would be out of the bank with two million dollars and on their way to Nuevo Laredo, Mexico, within the next five minutes.

Glancing at his wrist again—more for effect than to look at the time—Kauffman said, "I don't wish to be rude, Mr. Delano. But I am on a rather tight schedule. And frankly, toting two million dollars in cash out your door makes me a little nervous." He laughed, forcing a tension he didn't really feel into the sound. "The sooner I get the money into the buyer's hands and get the deed to the property signed over, the better I'll feel."

"I understand completely," Delano said, nodding. "I must say, it *is* a rather unusual transaction. Cash and all."

Kauffman shrugged. "It was the way the seller wanted it," he said.

"Tax reasons?" Delano asked.

Kauffman stared at him with a look that told the banker it was none of his business. "I didn't ask too many questions, Mr. Delano," he said. "Because due to the insistence on cash, I got the ranch at a great price."

Delano picked up on the look and quickly said, "My apologies. Banker's curiosity on my part, I'm afraid." He held a fist to his mouth and coughed. "Anyway, we have the cash on hand. As soon as the wire comes through..." His voice trailed off and he held up both hands and smiled again.

Kauffman stood up and reached for the phone on Delano's desk. "Do you mind?" he asked. Then, without waiting for an answer, he tapped the number to the Waters's home into the instrument and pulled a scrap of paper out of the side pocket of his gray jacket.

J.Travis Waters answered the call himself, as he'd been ordered. "This is Waters."

Quickly, enunciating clearly, Kauffman read off the number of his new account. "You have sixty seconds," he reminded the oilman, and hung up.

The last words caused Delano's eyebrows to rise again. "You *do* keep your people in line, don't you?" he said.

Kauffman was about to answer when he saw Washington suddenly twist in his chair and look toward the front lobby of the bank. He turned as well, and through the glass he saw a tall, rangy man wearing a straw cowboy hat and gaudy snakeskin boots. But it was not the hat or boots that caught his attention.

It was the uniform in between them.

Delano waved through the glass and the thin man walked in the open door. Once inside the bank president's office, Kauffman could read the shoulder patches on his arm. They stated for all to see that the man inside the uniform blouse worked for the New Braunfels Police Department. The name tag opposite the police shield on the man's chest read Coleman.

"Come in, Jim," Delano said. "These are the two gentlemen I mentioned to you earlier."

By now Washington, too, was on his feet. As the officer stopped and extended his hand in greeting, Kauffman took note of the ancient S&W .357 pistol in his holster. A second later, the phone on Delano's desk suddenly rang. The banker said, "Excuse me a moment," picked it up, identified himself, then turned as white as the papers littering his desk. Turning his attention back to Kauffman, Washington, and the New Braunfels cop, he said, "Jim, it's the FBI…they…" The rest of his words came out in an incoherent choke.

But Kauffman and Washington already had their Glocks out, the barrels shoved into both sides of the New Braunfels officer's ribs. "Hang up," Kauffman said. "Do it now or you both die."

Delano did as he'd been told.

"Sons of a bitches are faster than they used to be on those traces," Washington said in a low voice, dropping all pretense of being a businessman.

"Listen to me, and listen good," Kauffman said, his heart racing at this unexpected development. "We're all going to go back into the vault and get the money. My friend's and my guns will be out of sight to the rest of the employees. But they'll be in our hands and if either of you so much as sneeze at the wrong time we'll not only kill you but everyone else in the bank." He paused to let it all sink in, then said, "Do you understand?"

Delano and a very confused Coleman nodded.

"Wait a minute," Washington said. Then, after a quick glance through the glass to make sure no one in the lobby was watching, he unsnapped the retaining strap on the cop's holster and pulled out the revolver. Opening the cylinder and dumping the rounds onto the carpet, he replaced the weapon and then nodded at Kauffman.

Hiding their pistols under their suit jackets, Kauffman and Washington pushed Delano and Coleman out the door. "Big smile on both of your faces," Kauffman ordered in a whisper just before they passed through a low swing door to the rear of the cashiers' booths. Three women and two young men smiled back as they passed, none the wiser.

A moment later they had entered a rear office. Kauffman came in last and closed the door behind him. Both he and Washington produced their pistols again and Kauffman tapped Delano on the cheek with his. Nodding toward the thick vault door, he said, "Open it. And don't give me any crap about timers or combinations. You knew I was coming, you knew when, and you are ready."

Delano turned and twisted the rotary wheel on the vault door. A moment later, he used both hands to pull it open. Without being ordered further, he pointed to a pair of black canvas bags on the floor. "We got it ready for you," he said, his voice trembling slightly. "One million in each bag." Sweat had begun to pour down his forehead into his eyes, making him squint in pain. But he was either too frozen to wipe it away or feared raising a hand might be misinterpreted and get him shot. "Now, please…" he said. "Just take it and—"

Kauffman brought his Glock around in an arc and struck Delano squarely in the mouth. The chubby man fell to his side on the floor, just inside the vault. Blood spurted from his split bottom lip and tears began to form in his eyes.

Kauffman turned to Coleman. "Get in there with him," he said.

The cop followed the order without hesitation.

Washington jammed his Glock back into his belt and leaned into the vault, grabbing both bags and pulling them out into the office. Quickly, while Kauffman held the hostages at bay with his pistol, Washington unzipped both bags, verified that they did indeed hold cash, then nodded to Kauffman. Looking back into the vault, Washington said, "What do you want to do with them?"

Kauffman's nervousness over the unexpected FBI call was gone, and he felt a surge of pride and adrenaline now that the cards were falling his way again. "I think we'll leave them in the vault," he said quietly.

"Yes!" Delano said, finally wiping the sweat from his face. "Just close the door and it'll lock us both in. No one will even know what happened until long after you're gone!"

Kauffman stared at the overweight banker for a moment. Delano's face was a disgusting mixture of sweat, tears, blood and fear. Officer Coleman's confusion had disappeared and he looked frightened, too. Kauffman saw not men but symbols of everything that was wrong with America. One man represented those who had grown fat on the misery of the poor. The other had not only allowed it to happen, but persecuted those who tried to put a halt to that misery.

Without further thought, he raised his arm to head level and fired two shots.

As the roar inside the vault died down, Kauffman heard the jittery chatter on the other side of the office door. The tellers could not have missed hearing the shots. He and Washington would have to hurry.

Kauffman opened the office door again, then reached down for the handle of one of the black bags. "Let's go!" he said to Washington as he raced out into the tellers' area with the Glock in his other hand. The tellers had all congregated in the corner farthest from the vault. The women and one of the young men were crying. The other young man looked at Kauffman with a thousand-yard stare. None of them presented a threat.

Yet Kauffman could not resist firing a few rounds into their midst as he passed through the lobby.

Kauffman sprinted through the doors leading out to the parking lot, this time with no thought whatsoever about letting his black brother go first. Running to the van, he slid the side door open and threw the bag inside, then jumped up into the passenger's seat as Washington tossed the other million dollars in and then circled the vehicle for the steering wheel.

Ten seconds later, they were turning out of the parking lot and heading down the street. Kauffman pricked his ears. No sirens could be heard. "Let's go to Mexico," he said as he settled back against the seat.

Washington nodded his agreement as he turned onto the highway heading south toward San Antonio. "You remember what I said right before we went in back there?" he asked Kauffman.

"About this being a different kind of bank job?" Kauffman asked back, closing his eyes.

"Yeah," Washington said. "That."

"What about it?"

"I was wrong," Washington said as they left New Braunfels, Texas, and at least two more dead men.

16

Jack Grimaldi was far more than just a top pilot who could fly a plane through the eye of a needle. He was also a man who caught on quick, and he proved it the second the Executioner opened the door to the Learjet and said, "Jack, meet Petre Obregan."

Grimaldi twisted behind the controls of the plane and extended his hand. "Pleased to meet you," he told the Mexican. After a lightning-fast glance of understanding at the Executioner, he leaned forward and flipped a switch on the Stony Man Farm radio. Bolan knew he had just silenced any incoming calls to his and Obregan's ears. But Grimaldi would be able to pick them up on the headset wrapped over his brown suede bush pilot's cap.

Bolan had stowed both his and Obregan's suitcases in the luggage compartment before getting on the plane. Knowing that the green ammo box might draw unwanted attention from police or other officials who chanced to see it, he had wrapped the VX canisters in T-shirts to insulate them against accidental puncture, then stored them in a padded computer case. To anyone watching, it would appear he was simply one of the thousands of men who carried a laptop with them.

Taking his seat next to Grimaldi, Bolan watched Obregan buckle himself in behind the pilot. He still had the computer case with him, and he set it on the deck of the plane between the seats.

Grimaldi glanced over his shoulder at the bag. "What are we totin' boss?" he asked, staying in character as Anton Mikhailovich's pilot.

Bolan chuckled for Obregan's benefit. "Believe me, Jack," he said. "You don't want to know." He looked down at the case himself, then said, "Let's just say it's more important than ever that you don't crash us."

"That wasn't what I meant," the pilot said.

"I know what you meant," the Executioner replied. "But don't worry. According to my new friend here this is an in-country flight. We don't have to worry about customs on either side of the border."

"Like, *how* in-country?" Grimaldi said as he began flipping more switches and letting the Learjet warm up.

"Just barely," Bolan said. "Nuevo Laredo."

"Nuevo Laredo," Stony Man Farm's top pilot said in a western twang. "Always wanted to go there."

A few seconds later they were taxiing toward the runway, and a moment after that rising into the air.

The Executioner settled into his seat. In the reflection of the Learjet's windshield he saw Obregan watching the back of his head. Jimenez might finally trust him, but his right-hand man still didn't. Not that it mattered much at this point. One way or another, the game would soon be coming to a close.

Obregan didn't know it yet, but in a few hours he'd be dead.

As they rose to cruising altitude Bolan used the break in the action to sum up the situation in his head. Earlier, when Kurtzman had informed him about what was happening back in the States with the New Symbionese Liberation Army, he had decided to go after them as soon as he was finished with the Jimenez mission. Now, it appeared the two missions would be one and the same. With a little luck he could kill both birds with one stone. But he knew it would take more than luck—it always did. What it took to beat back the evil in the world, whether that evil came from drug dealers, terrorists, or any other type of criminal, was planning, skill, determination and a willingness to get down in the trenches and to fight such wrongdoers on their own level.

The Executioner was willing to risk it all.

Opening one eye, Bolan glanced at the computer case again. Rather than haul the dangerous nerve gas around with him, he would have preferred to have destroyed it and taken dummy canisters to the meeting with the New Symbionese Liberation Army. After all, they had no way to test the product without dying themselves. But whoever was calling himself Field Marshal Pentad knew the VX was coming disguised as Soviet-made pepper spray, and there was no time to slip away from Obregan's already suspicious eyes to create fakes. And like Jimenez himself had said, the NSLA men knew Obregan's face. Which meant the Executioner needed the gunman with him to insure that the deal went down smoothly—at least until the Executioner decided to rough it up.

His eyes still on the bag, Bolan realized he had only been

half-joking when he warned Grimaldi not to crash. If the plane went down and the canisters ruptured, all three men on board would die if the crash didn't kill them. Worse yet, if the crash occurred in a populated area it would also mean the deaths of dozens, hundreds, or maybe even more men, women and children. As it spread, the VX would dissipate and become harmless. But anyone within its lethal range would die in agony.

Bolan turned back to the windshield. Taking the gas along with him was a necessary risk. Missions were full of such risks, and it would do no good to dwell on it further. Looking back over his shoulder, he said, "Okay, Obregan. I know we're heading for Nuevo Laredo. Now, tell me the rest."

Obregan switched his stare from Bolan to the back of Grimaldi's head.

"It's okay," the Executioner said. "He can be trusted." He turned to look at the pilot himself. "He knows I'd kill him if he ever leaked anything. Don't you Jack?"

Grimaldi did a good job of faking fear. "You know it, boss," he said. "But you also know I'd never do that."

The act seemed to satisfy Obregan. "We will meet tonight with the head man of this New Symbionese Liberation Army himself," he said. "He calls himself Field Marshal Pentad."

"I already know that," Bolan said. "What's his real name?"

Obregan shrugged. "Who knows?" he said. "And who cares? The important part is that he will be bringing two million dollars in cash to buy the canisters."

"Where do we meet him?" Bolan asked.